Dedicated to Dode and Daisy Opp

THE
HOTEL
A NOVEL

KARL FOREHAND

TABLE OF CONTENTS

THE HOTEL

THE FLIMSY SCREEN DOOR MUST HAVE BEEN ADDED AS more of an afterthought. Why anyone would taint the glory of this entrance with this cheap attempt to repel flies, he would never know. He briefly noticed several layers of streaked paint, demonstrating man's desire to upgrade and renovate, instead of appreciating. The screen door nearly fell off its hinges as he opened it slowly, trying not to make a scene.

Joe Forester held his breath to marvel at the size and girth of the entrance door. He remembered restoring his own, similar to this one, earlier that year. The sheer weight of the oak was amazing, but this one adorned hand carved features that mesmerized. Was it protection from harsh, Midwestern winters or something else that caused the owners a century before to erect such a barrier between themselves and the outside?

Walking through the doorway of the 100-year-old hotel brought back memories of an earlier time in his life when things were simpler. The feel and smell of the old building reminded him of a dusty hardware store in his long-forgotten hometown. Scattered throughout the Midwest and South are remnants of once thriving towns such as this that converted and went the way of progress. Yet, somehow a few majestic old relics remain, and, like the elderly, they each have their own individual markings, wrinkles, scars that make them beautifully unique.

Joe craved to know archaic structures from that past. This one proclaimed a tall ceiling, ornately decorated, though the wallpaper cracked and peeled from years of water damage. Original hardwood floors bowed and rippled here and there. Every inch of the once stately

hotel indicated talented artisanship that was now sadly enduring vary-
ing levels of deterioration. Piles of dated décor sat as mini shrines to its
past grandeur and glamor. In dark corners, those mounds housed ver-
min and arachnids until taken out on the next trash day and removed
by a caring new owner. In some halls and rooms, framed black and
white scenes, patinaed sconces, and fragmented signage hung loosely
on walls, desperately clinging to a time never to be seen again.

Many similar buildings of the period had placards or etchings
showing their actual "birth" date, and this one was no different. An
oxidized brass plate announced the year "1912," though nothing
else on the exterior was worth noting. Endless remodels and facelifts
blended much like an old handmade sweater of a 90-year-old grandmother lacking the spare change to buy a new coat if she cared to do
so. The front porch was inviting, but uneven and slightly sagging.
There were traces of an awning which had long since fallen or been
removed. Like the façade, no one had the inclination or the means to
resurrect the ancient beauty. But, like all other parts of the hotel, there
was a story behind every wrinkle.

To the left was what could have been a type of lobby. He imagined
that it was the greeting place for the hotel as there was an antique bar-
like desk that formerly served as the center for everything in the hotel.
A corridor and a couple of rooms were visible in the distance, but this
was where everyone came to "get started" at this establishment. One
of the rooms behind this parlor was most likely an office, but for sure,
there was someone at this desk that granted entry and took money for
whatever you desired.

Based on other features in the room, the doorway on the right
possibly led down to some sort of underground storage space. An old
sign on the door long since faded into obscurity. He wanted to open
it, but something told him not to even take a peek. Scattered around
the room were compilations of dusty old relics that have survived simply because they told part of the story of the hotel and its past owners

and patrons. A faded picture, an old switchboard, and display cases harboring trinkets from days gone by all intrigued the observer even though some stories might never be known.

To the right of the front door was what remained of the old former parlor with only one piece of furniture and an old mirror. To the left, a stairway up to rooms above. Behind the parlor was an open room where one of the locals had been teaching karate. There were indications that this space may once have been an old ballroom or maybe formal dining for the hotel. Crumpled in the corner like a discarded soul, an old, dusty chandelier further confirmed his suspicions.

Another entry into and out of this room obviously connected to the restaurant, but it was closed tight. He noticed the well-worn pattern in the wood floor that led him to believe most people who came here also ate there. He wanted to see it, but he waited patiently for someone to escort him. Joe thought he heard the sounds of a dining establishment, but he quickly dismissed it, not wanting to arrive with any preconceived notions.

There was a rich story here. One to be told, Joe thought, and he wanted to know what it was. Some of it was obvious; the interior spoke partial truths but held secrets it was not yet willing to give up. He decided the residents kept some of them, too. The street that Joe lived on was named after the original owner, but much of this man's biography was confined to the typical monologue you find in a coffee table book smaller villages in the 50s had published to give an "official" rendition of the history they wanted to share. It was just about as accurate as whoever wrote the version wanted it to be. So, not only are unpleasant realities buried, but creative licenses are excuses to erect a façade much like the front of the building portrayed. It was ornate but crumbling—paint peeling, showing signs of age. Old stories are like that.

Joe had eavesdropped on a rumor that the hotel was haunted. He felt like he had progressed to the point of at least minimizing the

need for fearing something that might not even be real. His friend
was utterly convinced she once "felt something" like a cold breeze the
last time she went into the hotel. But, in his mind, he could quickly
rationalize the issue and an easy explanation erased all fear. Really,
the only thing he feared in this small town was gossip and retributive
folks when you get on their bad side. Movies tended to exaggerate
these kinds of things, and over the years, he had begun to see the
"other worldly" as something that more often resides inside us than
in a building.

Thus, walking into the hotel, he felt somewhat assured that he had
faced bigger "demons" and ghosts than whatever the past eras had left
here. That was until he met Marla. She emerged from one of the back
rooms. Immediately after an awkward introduction, she launched
into stories that were a little more detailed and caused his eyes to
widen just a bit, and his gut to rumble a little more than before.

Joe wasn't interested in narratives and spook stories. He just needed
to find an event space for events he aspired to create. He wanted to
help people heal from internal traumatic wounds. After leaving organized religion only a year prior and through his journey of healing, he
discovered some effective methods for leading others to identify past
trauma and begin to recover from it. He dreamed of holding retreats
for those that had experienced religious stress. This old hotel could
provide the perfect place to get away and do some of this altruistic
work.

He was dreaming of all these things when she appeared in front
of him.

MARLA

MARLA WAS JUST THE RIGHT MIXTURE OF PEOPLE. Everyone knew her and that made it almost impossible not to like her. She resembled that stereotypical aunt or grandma that loved baking cookies and telling stories. Her energy resonated like that of an explorer in a foreign land, and certainly the fact that she and her husband had bought the old hotel was at least an indicator of that. They were restoring—more like resurrecting—the old building room-by-room to provide some much-needed event space in a smaller town through its historic charm.

The new pandemic courtesy meant no handshakes, but Marla's warmth suggested that under normal circumstances he might have received a warm bear hug. Though an arranged appointment, both were startled to see each other. Somehow there was just enough mystery to the situation that made them both a little uneasy. Joe had been in downtown New York City corporate boardrooms and southern summer church meetings in cramped back rooms, so he wasn't intimidated, just a little out of his element. In this dark, cavernous space all the right smells and creaks and appearances not only remind him of the past but also instilled uncertainty about what would happen next.

Marla was a little breathless. Probably, a combination of whatever work she just abandoned and the walk to the front of the hotel, and the uneasiness from the various aspects of the situation.

"So, here it is!" she said, part apology and part invitation to share in her wonder and excitement. Her Midwest accent was thick with pride.

Joe's mother used to do that. She would start by telling people how she was proud of her work, then shift into pointing out the inadequacies of it before others noticed them or worse, sense she might be too prideful of what she had done. It was such a complicated mix of joy and shame and low self-esteem. He often wondered how much time she wasted wading through her own trauma and feelings of inferiority.

Joe had a thousand questions, mentally categorizing them through a hundred experiences of what was appropriate, what was necessary, and what would benefit him the most. That was one of the things that made conversation with him awkward. So instead, he just tried to coax his new friend to share what she knew about the space.

"So, tell me about the place."

Marla burst into a spectacular display of gesticulation about all she knew, only briefly pausing to clarify Joe's vision so that there weren't any misunderstandings. As she relayed the story of the renovation, she couldn't help whispering about the discoveries behind the tongue and groove. Apparently, Joe's future business was as a mixture of appealing rustic and American Gothic. So, a dented patinaed shovel hidden in a wall was more than just a Cracker Jack box surprise.

"So, I have heard the place is haunted," Joe asked without provocation.

He couldn't help himself. It was common knowledge, though no one explained why outright, and even though it didn't necessarily frighten him to think about it, it made everything a bit more edgy. Growing up in a small town, it was easy to demonize anything that people didn't understand. His grandmother often gossiped about the people down the road from her house because they didn't go to her church, and they didn't behave exactly like she did. Ironically, that same family considered her a witch because she was a little eccentric and refused to come to town except for toilet paper. A woman of the Great Depression, she relied on herself, her garden, and her grandson to take care of her. There's always a practical answer to ridiculous rumors, right?

"Oh, I know it is," Marla exclaimed almost immediately after the question left his lips. She had heard footsteps walking across the floor when there was clearly no one there. She just had a *feeling* someone was watching her. She saw something, someone, out of the corner of her eye in one of the back rooms.

Joe wondered what drove her to restore an old building that she insisted was a hostel of mystery. What could possibly be the motivation? Was she facing her fears, had she accepted an expensive dare, or did she just love a good challenge? Or perhaps she wanted to be part of the story. Joe knew the uneasiness of the unexplainable. He also knew the rush of adventures that didn't necessarily lead to preordained destinations. He had a suspicion that all journeys were like that.

"So, there is a basement?" Joe offered sheepishly knowing basements are by nature mysterious and dark and questionable, but he broached the subject anyway.

"Oh, I won't go down there!" There was no pretense in her voice. No dramatizing for effect. Marla drew a hard line on entering the basement.

Joe had heard the rumors of tunnels under the street. It was surreal for a town of 1,500 that this would ever be a reality. Even during Prohibition, it was so far-fetched to even imagine what secrets and treasures might be buried below his feet. A thousand stories—maybe one or two tragedies—possibly a revelation. But for now, it stayed hidden with the determination of a not-that-abnormal small-town woman who, like others, expressed the sentiment, "We don't go there."

"There's a rumor that a car is down there," she whispered, to maneuver the conversation away from whatever she was thinking before.

"Is that so?"

"Yeah, I believe the tunnel was wide enough for a car ... ," she trailed off as she turned to focus on some artifacts that had been preserved in the lobby.

Joe had reached his limit of direct curiosity because almost everything she said only caused him to have dozens more questions. It wasn't that he didn't want to know, but it seemed like he was sorting through junk in a garage. Picking a starting place would require a hot bath and some time to select just one thing he wanted to investigate further. He would look closer, but for now, he had reached his limit. It wasn't that he didn't enjoy this conversation, but his audible receptors kind of became fuzzy, and he couldn't focus on what she was saying.

Let's find a way to wrap this up.

Later Joe reckoned that she was discussing options for renting the space. He mentioned the rooms upstairs, where his friend had felt the "presence," but she dismissed it as a future option, and his mind trailed off again.

Most adventures start with plans that don't quite come to fruition as we imagined they should. This was no exception. The visit didn't provide many answers, only more questions. This was the beginning of something different because now he had more information that was both vague and specific enough to cause confusion. This, he reasoned, is what keeps people talking in small towns and sometimes what makes them keep quiet.

CHARLIE LACER

LATER THAT NIGHT, JOE STOPPED BY THE DOWNTOWN grocery store after work. Mary needed hairspray, so he quickly gathered a couple of toiletries and headed to the checkout. This grocery store was the small-town variety that he remembered from his youth, especially in his grandma's town. When he stayed with them on his birthday weekend, his grandpa always took him to have coffee and get farm supplies. They called it *trading* still, even though it was essentially just shopping.

There was a part of Joe that liked the convenience of urban life— stores where you can buy just about everything you could imagine. But another part of him (the introvert) liked the smaller spaces with less variety where you had to make do with less. It wasn't complicated, and it only took about two minutes to get to the nearest store, and there was never more than one person in the line. Also, in a small town, he could discover whatever is going on. Ask the barber. Question the cashier at the grocery store.

"Who would know about that old hotel? Who has that information?" he asked innocently.

The silent stare beckoned more information.

"I was wondering about the stories of tunnels and all underneath the streets. Who would know the history of stuff like that?"

The young girl's eyes rolled up, staring up at the ceiling like she hadn't thought about that in a while. Then, she suddenly motioned for Joe to punch a button on the credit card machine and asked if he wanted a receipt. After a second, he noticed who it was that appeared behind him.

Oh dammit. Charlie!

Of all the people who would show up now, why him? The last time they talked was on social media. Joe knew him as a rather decent person, but the discussion was around religion and that always tends to bring out the worst in people who felt like they have to prove a point, or save others, and it just gets a little personal a little too fast. He didn't have much against Charlie, he just didn't want to have a conversation with him.

"Oh, hey. I was curious who would know about the old hotel. It's not that important."

Being an introvert, Joe just didn't care for casual conversation, especially with people that were likely to start quoting Bible verses or inviting him back to church. He had been a deacon for 25 years and then gradually walked away. He'd had enough of trying to convince people of the "right way," and most of those conversations he later would regret.

"I don't know who would know," Charlie offered. "Maybe Tim Zeffernan."

"I don't know him," Joe said looking down and trying to move away, "Have a fine night, folks."

Despite all his time in high school debate, Joe still felt like a buffoon publicly speaking to anyone, especially when it was someone he didn't want to talk to. He was not adept at feigning emotions. He supposed that made him a more genuine person, but often people interpreted him being weird or just an ass.

After he got home, he told his wife about the encounter.

"Sometimes, they can tell you the genealogy of a person's family they barely know, and then other times they act like they just moved into town and don't know anything about anyone," Mary offered.

"I know, right? It's like everyone has heard of these tunnels but no one has ever seen them."

"They sure knew about us when our daughter had a glass of wine on her 21st birthday!"

Mary flustered over that time when Joe was called into the church office for a meeting. It was one of those group interventions where someone was "concerned" about a fellow member. She and their oldest daughter had gone out for a drink at a winery, then posted it on Facebook. The wrong person saw it and caused a stink. It wasn't that the pastor was totally against drinking, but they were worried how it would look with Joe being a deacon and all.

In many ways, that was the beginning of the end for Joe and Mary concerning organized religion. It was enough pressure just living in a small town where everyone knows your business, but small-town church can be the best and the worst of that world. If anything happened, they were the best at caring for each other. When nothing was happening, it was almost like they didn't have enough to do and needed to constantly be in other people's business. Eventually, Joe and Mary became disillusioned and separated from the theology they knew as children. They were comfortable with their evolving beliefs, but over the years grew apart from the church and the trauma that sometimes came along with it.

"Either someone knows a secret, or they just want to be the only one to know," Mary bellowed from the kitchen.

It was strange to Joe, but it wasn't a new thought. Why do people know so much about things that don't matter, things that aren't their business? Possibly, people are interested in different things. Some people can tell you what kind of tree is growing in your front yard whether you asked to know or not. Joe never cared much about those kinds of things or those kinds of people.

Joe's mind wandered back to the last decent conversation he had with Charlie—whether to go to church or simply the belief in God was enough. Why did anyone need religion in this day and age? The patronizing began and ended when Charlie's questions of Joe's beliefs concluded in a subliminal *"dumb ass"* comment. Joe didn't necessarily regret the argument, although he longed not to be weak enough to react to things like that. People say stupid things all the time.

Maybe I should apologize and just go talk to Charlie about the hotel.

Something in him knew that he knew more than he assumed. Betraying trust is a huge deal in a small town and there was something to be said about being the insider. Joe also knew within that two-minute span of leaving the store and entering his home, several discussions of his minute public conversation were replayed over internet, phone, or text. Most likely one or more of those conversations originated from someone on the second or even third aisle over.

He tried not to think about the dynamics of a small town too much, especially since he no longer warmed the Sunday pew. Now, he worried less about what people thought. However, he also knew that things could get complicated quickly when people misunderstood or took upon themselves to solve problems that didn't need solving.

"I think I'll go to the library tomorrow," he yelled over his laptop as he fruitlessly searched the internet for any history of the hotel but to no avail. "Want to go out to the porch?"

He and Mary, his now 30-year-bride, loved to sit on their wrap-around porch and light some torches. She loved to burn sage to cleanse herself after a long day of nursing and caring for others. It relaxed her, but they joked about the neighbors probably thinking they were smoking weed. They laughed about it often, but he knew things like that were only too close to being true to completely ignore.

Joe caught a glimpse of the stars as his mind wandered back to Prohibition and what the town might have looked like during those tumultuous years. They didn't talk about anything until he saw Mary blow out the flames and heard her remind him to come in.

He hoped this wouldn't be an obsession, but somehow, he knew it would be.

THE LIBRARY

BEFORE BED, VISIONS OF THE 1930S RAN THROUGH HIS head. What role would Joe have played in such a time of need and desperation? Would he have been the religious zealot condemning the masses for their secret lives or been wrapped up in the frivolity and wildness of bootlegging? He realized that choices made are subtle and any one of them can lead us down an alternate path. The owner of the hotel, George Popper, made a series of wise decisions in life. Well, at least financially.

Joe thought about the basement, which he could only picture as a swamp. It was probably flooded and mildewed; however, like other explorers, he couldn't help but wonder what was buried there. He chased several rabbit trails in his mind to no avail since he barely had enough information to imagine an elaborate tale. It was like he had traveled to a foreign country—everything was new and different and wondrous so that he couldn't focus on one idea long enough to form a coherent story. He fell asleep grasping at bits and fragments of the possible narratives.

Saturday morning came with anticipation of hopefully finding some answers in the library. The 9:00 a.m. alarm was early for some but not Joe. The switch from salaried to hourly employment had led to schedules that forced him to arise between 4:00 and 5:00 a.m. Oddly enough his body adjusted quickly and now he found himself awake at 4:30 every morning whether he wanted to get up or not. This also meant that he went to bed earlier than ever before, so as much as he still wanted to be a night owl, he couldn't. Similar to that new nightly urge to pee in the middle of the night, there was barely anything he could do to change it.

So, he sat down and wrote a new chapter in his blog. Hardly anyone read it, but a few took time to appreciate his thoughts about religion and struggling with understanding God in a new light. He could
have mass-released his writing to all the people that followed his old
denomination's teaching, but some of his views had changed enough
that most of them didn't speak to him, much less read his *heretical*
thoughts. By the time he scheduled the article to publish the following Thursday, the clock only read 6:00 a.m.

He had secured another meeting with Marla, so he scrawled some
questions in his journal to ask her later that day and some objectives
for the visit to the library.

6:10, dang!

He had nothing to do and three hours in which to do it. Scrolling
through social media had become a pastime but wasn't that interesting
today. He tried searching the web *again* to no avail. Strange. Reportedly
the hotel was the "best place within a hundred miles" to stop when
driving through this region. Was it possible that those famous Google
algorithms were too busy trying to distract Joe with the current hotel
ads than actually providing the information he wanted?

Mary still slept in. She was determined to stay under covers on
her days off and when using any of her coveted vacation days. *Her*
schedule had not changed in over 30 years. *Her* body woke up at 6:00
a.m. under normal circumstances. However, dealing with the virus at
work had drained her beyond normal. So, it was easy to allow her the
rest and venture alone on another one of his treasure hunts. Whether
it was the quest for religious favor or the search for a trophy buck, she
genuinely supported him. He often wondered how marriages survive
without that compromise. She was still sleeping soundly an hour later
when he got his third cup of coffee and decided to meditate.

Joe always paused before meditation and thought about this practice. Five years ago, he would have been apt to condemn anything
that sounded like *new age*, not for any intellectual reason other than

it just wasn't normalized in his former traditional faith. Over the years he sampled stress-relievers like yoga and mindfulness, and he gained insight from all over the world that people of all belief systems had discovered common threads that were helpful not only to their spirituality, but also to their physicality and emotional health. He was looking for an effective strategy and was surprised to discover so many were not religiously-based—they were considered "practices" and that intrigued him.

This morning's mindfulness practice enabled him to be present and accepting and grateful. It conveniently removed Joe's need to pace the floor waiting for the library doors to open and gave him actual data to focus on. The leftovers in the fridge distracted him enough to abandon his waning attempt at centeredness. So, he gave in and sloughed off to throw together a makeshift breakfast. He poured a fourth cup of coffee, even more refreshing than the first, and he paused to inhale the aroma as he took his vitamins, gazing out the back window at a squirrel scampering about in the leaves.

He fell into the comfort of his favorite chair, tapped to start a new podcast, and soon he was listening without paying attention as he ate. His mind wandered instinctively to the hotel and all the questions that still were unanswered. He resented the fact that he had spent three hours distracting himself from what his mind (and heart) desired. For just a moment he considered how that resonated with the rest of his life. How many hours, days, years had he wasted just filling up his time with things to do? Why couldn't he accept the challenges of some mystics to simply be present? What did that even mean and why was it important?

He was learning the answer to some of these questions. Wiser inquiry can lead to more mystery and paradox and nuance. He liked that this new world he was discovering brought him new peace outside of his certainty. But he realized not only that he was on some kind of journey but also, he was a long way from home. His tradition hadn't allowed for much exploration or questions. There was no time for that. This now four-and-a-half-hour excursion early in the day was just part of the adventure that he was on. It wasn't scheduled. It didn't have well-defined boundaries or objectives. Nonetheless, he was slowly learning to appreciate these times of solitude.

Joe startled the dog when he kicked the footrest down and jumped from his seat.

9:05, dang he was late.

Wait, why am I late? It's not an appointment.

He argued with himself as he slipped on a pair of jeans and his favorite button up shirt and hurried out to warm the car only later realizing he hadn't shaved or trimmed his beard. That would have been something he could have done in the over four hours he spent waiting to leave. Oh well, he eventually realized that the part of him that wanted to be organized and perfect was giving in to the part of him that was learning to be authentic. It was still a battle, but even that was a necessary part of the journey.

"To the library," he called triumphantly like he was taking the town by storm.

It was only a minute's drive to the library but too far to walk in the freezing cold, and he knew he would think of something else he needed to do when he got downtown.

As was his custom, he didn't waste much time on small talk with the librarian. She knew who Joe was even though they had never met. He realized he had thoughts about the sexy uptight librarians in the movies that take their hair down and transform into a raging, lustful animal right there in the library. He was embarrassed when he had these kinds of thoughts for a wide variety of reasons, but more so as this keeper of the classics was warm, welcoming, and generally his daughter's age.

She led him back to the *Genealogy* section and removed a large, white notebook from the shelf. She had done a little pre-research after

his initial call and said she couldn't find much of anything except this
ledger with the hotel owners' last name embossed on the cover. It
was a collection of mostly newspaper articles and census information
for people with the last name of Popper. She pointed to the "George
Popper" section and left him alone. It was extremely easy to piece
together the entire timeline of all the available information in about
an hour.

1912—*The hotel was opened by a relative of Mr. Popper's wife.*

1922—*George Popper purchased the hotel and renamed it Hotel
Popper.*

1933—*Popper remodeled parts of the hotel including the basement and new rooms upstairs.*

1960s—*The hotel was closed for about a year due to an interesting story.*

1970s—*When the interstate was built nearby; traffic was diverted
from the town; eventually the hotel was closed.*

1980s—*A couple of resurrection attempts for the hotel didn't take
hold … the story ends*

Yet, for Joe the story was only beginning.

He read a few interesting twists to the story. George and Mrs.
Popper had paid everyone's utility bill one month which created noto-
riety but also some consternation. Most were thankful; some resentful. When newspapers summarized the hotel's activities, they mentioned notable guests who had stayed there, which wasn't unusual for
50 years of history. Mrs. Popper was quoted as saying, "we housed the
best and the worst of them." Joe took this also with a grain of salt.

There were other interesting pieces of information such as George's
father died of an "accidental" shotgun blast to the back side of his
head—apparently, Bud slipped and fell. At age 24, George was reported
to be in a noteworthy, two-hour wrestling match with someone from

across the river. It also appeared as though every attempted business venture was fruitful to some degree. From farming to hunting supplies to hotel management, he prospered at most everything he put his hands to. To make the story even sweeter, he appeared to be quite generous later in mid-life, endearing him to most town folk. He discovered, however, that some of the residents didn't appreciate the couple paying their utility bill. Why? It wasn't clear.

For Joe, something just kept creeping into his consciousness. The initial thought was why is there nothing about the hotel, about Mr. Popper, in all the county history? Most of these books were assembled by residents at one time or another, but why, in a book of landowners and pictures of their properties, would Bud Popper be noted but not the owner of a hotel for 50 years? And why were there no pictures of the inside of the hotel? Nowhere! In this book of family history and articles about the man, why were there no pictures of his business or any events that happened in the hotel?

Joe's middle daughter often complained that there weren't many pictures of her in their family albums. She joked that she was probably adopted. He knew the truth, but even in her short life, there were hundreds of images of her in various places, even before "googling" was a term. It was just a prevailing thought. Just this one book, some long gaps in history, only a few pictures from the sixties, no pictures of the hotel. Either it was the oddest of coincidences or something was awry.

He noted these questions for Marla. He had a few hours to spare until he could get more answers, so here he was again trying to learn how to just be. He returned home just in time for the noon game. Football was limited lately because of the virus, but he forced himself to watch a game that didn't interest him to pass some time. The image of George stuck with him. He seemed like a typical-looking, Midwestern guy. Glasses, overalls, a little too much sun exposure, losing some of his hair. Most people in the area claim to be of German descent—some were, some weren't. This guy definitely was.

After more wasted time, he left his cozy chair and his now woke wife to seek more truths. On the way to the hotel, Joe bought some flashlight batteries. He knew what he wanted to ask Marla, but even more so, he knew what he wanted to see.

EXPLORATION

MARLA WAS IN THE LOBBY PUTTING UP CHRISTMAS DECOrations for a pop-up vendor that was due to arrive in a few days. Joe startled her a little with his entrance and assumed she must live somewhat on edge all the time. Her belief that the hotel was haunted, and the nature of an old building probably keep her with a buzzing level of adrenaline. Maybe that was why she bought it in the first place. Sometimes in a small town, you have to create your own excitement. That thought was a warning sign to Joe, but he, too, suffered from the same malady: always looking for an adventure.

For this visit, Marla invited him to take a chair. He went through the timeline and what he discovered at the library. Most of the information she confirmed, although some she had never heard before. He felt satisfied that he was up to speed about most of what the new owner knew about George Popper and Hotel Popper. He didn't know what she had discovered in her own treasure hunting. He verified things she had told him previous and took some notes, but what he wanted to do was look around for himself.

Joe needed to know why Marla didn't go into the basement. She told the story of the last time she was down there and saw a man standing in the corner. Her husband had been in the lobby waiting for her, and she had run right past him and straight out the front entrance. In Joe's mind, her description sounded a lot like the owner, but he let her describe the entire situation and didn't inquire any further questions. Whether it was what she saw or what she thought she saw was kind of irrelevant. It was her experience, and he didn't doubt her interpretation.

Joe asked to see the upstairs first. He reasoned that he might as well start with the tamer of the two uncharted territories. She led him up the original staircase. The descriptions in the newspaper alluded to a more magnificent hotel than what he observed. The hotel was reported to be the best place in this part of the country for those traveling between urban areas. But the stairway resembled more like the steps to grandma's attic than a majestic entrance. They were covered in dirty, dark orange shag carpet. Right away, Joe noticed that almost everything he saw was not from the 1920s, but from later years.

Just along the walls leading to the entryway to the rooms were what appeared to be stored collections of various, random articles. Marla easily removed the plywood that boarded this floor. Joe felt privileged to be allowed into these catacombs. It was apparent that there had been pilfering, possibly for copper wiring or other valuables, and the disheveled state had the appearance that someone had been frantically looking for something. Original mattresses and the small, individualized rooms preserved much of the original intention.

It was what he expected, only much more overwhelming. The accumulation of junk was almost astronomical. He didn't have time to think about the stories of haunting because of the sheer mass of visual cues he was receiving. There were small patches of wallpaper, different layers of revealed carpet and hardwood floors. The furniture was mostly 1970s, mixed with antiques from a much earlier date. And, almost without reason or order, there were piles of random boxes, books and items that could have been left there yesterday.

"It was right here," she said as they neared the end of the long hallway.

A paranormal team had investigated this area and heard a voice right about where Joe imagined his friend's story took place. He allowed for the possibility, just like the "man" in the basement. He was not heavily invested in being right or wrong, judging against his own understanding. He loved that about his separation from organized religion. He didn't have to always be right anymore; he could just explore.

Marla always said something mysterious into the conversation just when Joe was starting to get a grasp. When they were nearing the stairs, she casually said, "There's the other part."

"Wait. What other part?"

"It's the other half of the property," she said as she nodded her approval to proceed down the narrow hallway.

The other side of the upstairs was almost identical in size. It was almost completely covered with books from God knows where and gave the appearance that it was once divided into rooms. But what were they for? Like most of the property, someone had accumulated in mass and stored it randomly. This time it was mountains of books that didn't have a particular purpose except as objects to hoard. Joe wondered why we have this tendency. We buy spaces and then fill up those spaces, like the barn's parable in the Bible.

At this point, it was enough for Joe to assume this might once have been meeting rooms or classrooms, but after a few more questions about the space, Marla said, "Yeah, this is over the large ballroom downstairs."

There's another part of the hotel? Why didn't we talk about this before?

After several minutes of perusing the area, they returned to the first level. Marla motioned to the back of the hotel to the sprawling ballroom. She disappointed him by halting his curiosity stating the area was not available at this time. Joe's introverted nature kicked in and knew he was running out of small talk energy. His inquisitive host had already begun the initial personal questions that usually led to nosy prying; thus, he didn't pursue information about the mysterious ballroom. Maybe next time. Instead, he focused on his intended target of the day.

Joe asked sheepishly if they could see the basement. Joe had imagined a swampy, wet horror show that scared him enough to not even want to continue, but after she agreed, he found something quite different. It appeared to be the same size as the first side of the hotel and much like most other basements he had seen in this part of the world. Lots of shelves and lots of neatly organized junk! It was like one in a house he rented recently, only it was ten times the size and much more populated with everything you could imagine.

There were pockets of interest, like a dark room and pottery collection, but most of what he saw were from recent decades and recent owners. Sadly, nothing resembled the recreation room he read about or the speakeasy stories he imagined.

"I saw *him* there," Marla pointed out to a dark part of the maze.

It *could* likely be a place for a ghost to hang out and observe, but no ghost today. She showed him where the tunnels *could* have been, but a century is a long time, and there had been several renovations, some raised cement and brickwork along with more junk neatly piled in front of everything. He was nearly overwhelmed by the sheer volume of visual stimuli.

"I think the buried car is on the other side of that wall."

There was a utility tunnel, much smaller than most rumors he had heard. It was a part of a cement wall that ran the length of the hotel. Just like the ballroom above, this part of the hotel was sealed off from the rest. The cement was hand detailed and somewhat rough. It wasn't necessarily unusual for a basement, but with all the other details, it caused just enough wonder to send the mind off on a "what-if" journey. Joe's mind was exhausted, and he started making his way to the old staircase.

He was thankful that the two things he wanted to explore were not like he had imagined. He didn't encounter anything too spooky, and he never felt in danger, just disappointed that he only got to the edge of what he wanted to discover. Case in point, the last thing she showed him was a flower bed outside the south side of the hotel. Apparently, the flower bed covered up the steps that led down to an original tavern that no one knew about. Just to make it even more fascinating, the original name was "The Snake Den" or something like that. As you might have guessed, he hadn't read about this at the library.

So, at the end of the day, Joe was glad that he answered some questions related to the timeline. He didn't feel a need to disprove or prove the paranormal aspects, but he appreciated the fact that it made everything more interesting. He did feel the age-old frustration every explorer feels. After setting out on a journey of discovery, we have to first work through the inevitable let-down that occurs when the journey is not as we imagined. He was somewhat defeated that everything he wanted to see was just on the other side of a wall or buried just a little deeper.

Here we go, he thought as he got back in his car.

Marla was still talking to him, but his conversation allotment was way over budget for the day. He knew he was at a critical point. The point where you realize this is going to be harder than imagined. *It's not what I thought* and *I'm going to invest more time and some money and I'm not going to stumble upon anything,* and *I must go in search of it.* It's the point where you abandon the path you are on and return home or step outside the boundary and make a new path.

He didn't move forward for a couple of days. He just spent any spare time he could muster processing what he saw and what he learned. Joe was surprised at all the emotional thoughts he had about George Popper. Anything he could have surmised, he did. How did Bud Popper actually die? Did the owner of the hotel have something to do with it? Was George connected with the Mob like some say and others deny? Why did everything work out for him? Was it because he had some help? And that wrestling match that lasted two hours? You have to have quite a temper to fight that long. Is that how he kept all the businesses going his way? Or was he a community-minded, benevolent man who genuinely loved everyone?

Without any direct evidence, all Joe could do was make assumptions and guesstimations. Why did he care anyway? He felt that little inkling to quit, but he resolved to take on one more pursuit and check with the expert that Charlie had said might know something.

Oh, boy! Those kinds of guys are talkers, and Joe would have to endure the excruciating exercise of hearing all this guy's non-related stories or whatever he thought was interesting to finally get to the morsel of truth that made it all worthwhile. He considered it his sacrifice—this might help him decide whether to abandon the journey or move ahead— and he wasn't really optimistic, just a little hopeful.

ORIGINS (CIRCA 1975)

WHENEVER JOE THOUGHT ABOUT EXPLORING, HE thought about his brothers. In those times, parents would let the kids go outside and play, and they invented things to do until it was time to come in for supper. He and Marty would spend the entire day on adventures in the summer until their mom tracked them down, or more accurately, when they got so hungry, they had to come home to refuel.

Some might propose that it was a much safer time for kids to run freely, but honestly, it was that his family couldn't even afford a decent television—there were only about 5 channels anyway. Video games were not exactly obsessions, and there just wasn't anything else to do except go outside and invent something. Joe learned how to steal candy during those years when he attended a private Christian school. So, it wasn't that the times were morally better, they just were what they were.

In his neighborhood, drainage ditches became prevalent. In warmer climates, they dried up and following them could ultimately lead to adventure. Joe and his brothers and whoever else tagged along were in a world of their own. Petty theft and minor vandalism were always a possibility, but the nature of the adventure was always to see what they discovered. Mostly they were hungry to find something they had never seen before.

Joe was in no way equipped to deal with the low level of anger he felt. Corporal punishment was popular in that era in the evangelical circles his parents ran in. Looking back, he couldn't point to anything positive that came from all the spankings. It just made him a little angrier and a little less understood. But nursery workers, parents and teachers could all release their anger when he misbehaved or just disagreed with them. He channeled all that negative energy into the primary positive he found in life—his summer adventures.

One of his schoolmates lived on the edge of the subdivision across from the public middle school. They had nicer playground equipment than his private institution, and that simple fact is what lured them across the street one day. But it wasn't the monkey bars or slides that thrilled them. For these boys, it was the simple act of following each other to wherever looked fun.

Something out in the nearby field caught their eye, and they would pursue it. "Hey, what is that?" became the mantra for further discovery. The playground led to the field which led to the old tractor which led to the creek filled with crawdads and other live creatures. They followed it for about a half-mile, turned over rocks that hid the palm-sized crustaceans, and dodged the occasional water snake that would dart out from its sanctuary causing them to reevaluate their mission until they could muster some more courage to continue on. Eventually, the creek led them to a pond.

Looking back, Joe couldn't imagine jumping into the murky pool especially after witnessing his own children do the same in a nearby cattle pond, then resurface covered in leeches. He fought the gag by thinking about probable manure, urine, and who knows what else that stewed there. Mary most likely burned their clothes and spent the rest of the night disinfecting, bathing, and inspecting her children for foreign pests that still might be present. She was originally from New England and some of this was just a little too much to bear.

Joe and his brothers were relentless in their pursuit of adventure. The drainage ditch eventually led them to a busy intersection. The storm tunnel across from their school opened up into another cavern that led them under the street to an area where water could drain down into the cistern and be swept away to their favorite place to explore. This was a major find because it was a combination of a place to investigate, a makeshift clubhouse, and a place to plan other adventures. It also became a place to torment passing motorists. They tried the old dollar bill on a string, but none of the cars above noticed it, so they changed strategies. They tried throwing water balloons, but it was too hard to hit passing cars without being noticed. One day, Joe found a long narrow pipe and had a brilliant idea.

"What if we jabbed this up into the bottom of the cars?" he proposed.

Their silent smiles let him know that they were considering the devious plan but needed more information. Like most children, it was common not to think everything through. This was a point several adults reminded them of from time to time. Yet, not thinking too much was exactly what made the adventure worth doing. Like this one, some of them were hilarious!

"When a car pulls up to the stop sign, I'll jab this rod up into the bottom of his car, and they won't know what is happening. It's going to be hilarious!" Joe continued.

That was plenty of information for the plan to take wings. They waited patiently for the car to pull over the grate built into the road. They could hear the engine running, were probably inhaling exhaust, but they didn't worry about minor things like that. Joe found a hole just wide enough to slip the pipe through. He gripped it tightly and rapidly raised and lowered it, striking the motorists' undercarriage with almost a little too much vigor. The *boom, boom, boom* echoed throughout their underground chamber as the driver began to pull away and then screeched to a halt.

"That was awesome," Marty said as they heard the cussing and carrying on above, wondering what just happened. Joe and his companions ducked back into the shadows trying to conceal their belly laughs which emerged from a bit of fear and sheer delight over this current activity that would entertain them for at least a couple of hours. It was probably close to time to go home before something happened that changed the nature of the game.

Up to that time, the motorists would screech to a halt, open their car doors, and start frantically discussing and investigating only to drive away confused. But this time the motorist didn't drive away. Perhaps he was a repeat customer or just a little more observant than the others, or he caught a glimpse of the boys in the grating—who knows. There was about a minute of silence before the man appeared in the entryway to the tunnel, about fifty feet away. He couldn't see the boys, but it was clear that he was over-the-top angry.

"I know you're down there! If I didn't have the kid in the car, I'd come in there!"

He continued with his rant for several minutes. His white pants were soaked with the murky water from the tunnel, and he appeared to be sweating profusely. The boys knew enough about angry adults that it was better just to be quiet at this point. Any bright ideas they had were squelched, hoping this chapter of the story would be over soon enough as long as they were hidden and quiet. Eventually, the guy left. They waited for him to drive off, then they waited a few more minutes before they chuckled nervously to themselves and made their way out to the entrance.

Recently, Joe mentioned this event when his siblings gathered for a family birthday. It is still a highlight of he and Marty's lives. The story lives on. His brother remembers it even more vividly than he does. Maybe because he was more terrified or traumatized by it.

As he grew older, Joe struggled to adapt to the world around him. Eventually, he probably became more like the guy in the white pants than the kid under the street. But he never forgot what it felt like to be in the middle of an adventure. He would return to that feeling several times in his life. He would feel it about 40 years later in Asia, and he was feeling inklings of it now thinking about Hotel Popper. Tunnels under streets made him think of that afternoon when he and his gang drove motorist's crazy for two hilarious hours.

He knew this much: Too much planning will kill the adventure. He learned that especially from a couple of failed vacations. The things he planned often didn't come to fruition and only frustrated himself and his companion. The real adventures came by following the clues and investigating the "what is that?" moments as they unfolded.

He was in that posture—waiting for the next clue—when the phone rang.

THE PHONE CALL

THAT SUDDEN SOUND BLAST ALWAYS STARTLED HIM. MOST people wanting to get in touch with Joe usually emailed or sent a text. It was the way of the world, and he loved it. Being an introvert, he didn't care for talking on the phone, though he knew it was occasionally necessary. He almost sent it to voicemail, but he noticed it was a local number, and he was waiting to hear about a job opportunity, so he answered, reluctantly.

"Hello," he always tried to be positive, but his voice never carried like he wished it would.

"Joe. This is David Sidebaum, I heard you were looking into the hotel and tunnels and such."

"Oh, yes, you must be the guy that Charlie mentioned," Joe offered.

"Charlie, Charlie who? No, that's not who I heard it from, and I can't stand that guy anyway. I was just calling to tell you ... just leave it alone."

Joe was stunned, but this kind of call wasn't unusual. He experienced it once or twice a year in the church. He supposed it was common to most community organizations. There is always an undercurrent of control. Even when the stakes are low, people are afraid that things won't be like they imagined or not like they want them to be. They go to astounding lengths to control the circumstances. It is not as much a quest for power as a response to their somewhat unrealistic fear of what might happen. After all, if we allow A, then B is bound to happen and possibly even C or D.

"Wait, what?" Joe answered. "Leave what alone? I'm simply curious about the history of the hotel. It is an interesting story! Wouldn't people in town like to know the real history of the town?"

"There's no need to pull scabs off old wounds," David continued.

"Old wounds? Are there old wounds? Why wouldn't we want to talk about those things?"

This was another familiar conversation from church. Many middle-aged men in the Midwest carry around a fair amount of trauma, but the last thing they want to do is talk about it. They might have tried that once, but it was too painful, and it didn't help. The argument was not about pulling scabs. The argument was that they were ignoring there was still a scab, so there must still be some unhealed trauma. But trying to discuss these types of things was like bumping into someone with that exposed scab on their arm and watching them react instead of respond. It never went well.

The part of leaving church that Joe regretted was not the things we might imagine. The part that troubled him the most was that there were still wounded people in the church that preferred to bypass their grief and trauma instead of dealing with it. He believed in miracles and such, but often church people opt for avoiding the issue rather than enduring the hard work of recovery. Hardly anyone in the church wants to hurt people, but the system often facilitates moving on, just like David wanted him to do. Smaller towns are often a lot like smaller churches, and sometimes they're tightly connected.

"Do you know anything about the tunnels?" Joe pitched as a Hail Mary, hoping David would intercept and tell what he knew.

"Listen, Joe, leave it alone. I don't know where you came from, but around here we let sleeping dogs lie, we don't poke them with a stick. You don't want to get bit, do you? Enough said!"

Joe listened to the silence for a few seconds and his cell phone kind of automatically hung up. He saved the number into his phone under "David" … What was his last name? Oh well, he just entered "David the Ass" and figured he wouldn't forget him; he was vaguely like many people he knew. What was with this guy? Why couldn't adventure ever be smooth? Why couldn't his church build a new facility without getting into arguments? Why can't we even go on a short vacation without unforeseen circumstances making things more complicated?

Part of him knew the answer, but he didn't want to concede the point yet, so he just sidestepped and went on cursing David the Ass for a few more minutes. Of course, Mary agreed with him, but steadily she was gaining a voice, and he didn't know how long he would have a partner that always agreed with him. Again, part of him liked that—part of it just made him angry.

Just about the time Joe calmed down and focused his attention on a football game, the phone rang again. This was one of things he and Mary could always agree on. It was somehow soothing. He had played high school football and could always envision himself as a running back even though his 5.0 speed would have never made the cut. Joe wasn't sure why Mary liked football because she didn't even understand the rules all that well. Maybe it was the tight pants or the colorful uniforms. Most likely, it was because her mother also liked football, and it brought up memories of earlier times.

"Hello," Joe squawked, annoyed.

"Joe, it's Charlie. I talked to the guy at Bible study, and he doesn't know that much about the hotel. He focused his interests on other parts of history. He said he's heard about all that stuff but never seen it or seen much evidence."

"Yeah, I know, I didn't find much either," Joe offered, hoping he could somehow spark some interest.

"Listen, it's not worth the time. Why not let sleeping dogs lie?" Charlie said rather seriously.

He realized what had probably happened. David wouldn't just have warned Joe about poking around. He would have taken as many steps as possible to make sure this little thing was put to rest. In the mind of some people in small towns, things go something like this: "We kind of like our town the way it is. Anything that might upset this is seen more like a cancer or demon that needs to be exercised." Most people there would never hurt anyone physically, they just don't know how to deal with the unreasonable fear they have that someone is going to upset or steal or take what they treasure.

"Come on Charlie, I swear I just want to satisfy my curiosity," Joe begged.

"Maybe you should get back in church and set your mind on things that matter."

Joe washed over in temporary anger, followed by a deep sadness he felt for religion and the church. Shaming and belittling was customary practice when people didn't take the time to talk about what was really bothering them. During his years in the church, he noticed there had never had time to discuss what was wrong or troubling—it was just a thing that was not worth the effort. It was a sleeping dog they didn't want to awaken, and it was all connected.

"Thanks for your time, Charlie," Joe said dismissively.

"No problem, Joe, maybe we'll see you next week?"

"Talk to you later," Joe said and almost didn't finish speaking before he hung up.

Now he was angry! This kind of crap is what made him want to move to a larger town and just blend in. He wouldn't be aware of the history of the city, and he wouldn't care. He could just let the whole thing carry him along, and he'd just be a cog in someone else's wheel. He thought about this often but was never able to convince himself that he could do it long term.

Joe paced the porch before abruptly announcing to Mary, "I'm going down to the library again."

She glanced up from the computer, most likely indulging in something related to the grandchildren or possibly hospital files she only found time to review at home. He admired her hard work and dedication and love for her family, but his primary focus was, "Why does it have to be difficult? Why can't anything be easy? Why do people keep secrets?" He briefly thought about the sleeping dogs in his own life but brushed them aside, or more accurately, pushed them down. A part of him knew that he had some similar issues as the town, but he didn't allow himself to connect the dots presently. He was on a mission!

He again waved at the librarian who sat too engrossed in a novel— a cove pictured on the cover and probably something to do with Maine—to notice his return. He made his way back to the white notebook, storming past more than a few raised eyebrows, to find the Popper book once more.

He flipped through the yellowing pages at warp speed. It wasn't in any way a pace that would prove fruitful, but he was verifying his suspicions, and when he was in that mode, he wasn't apt to slow down and probe further. He was just confirming what he already knew.

"Nothing," he said to himself. "There is nothing here for over 20 years and no pictures!"

For the longest time, he just stared at the dull gray wall. His mind was stuck on the same few thoughts:

There are no pictures!

If everyone knows about the tunnels, why hasn't anyone seen them?

If this guy was such a saint, why so much white space in history?

If the hotel was such an amazing place to stay, why is there no record?

Why won't people talk about it, what are they hiding?

Repeat.

It startled him when the older gentleman spoke to him from the doorway, "Maybe I could help you with your inquiry?"

The man was dressed in a button-up shirt under new overalls. Simple and comfortable Oxfords gave an air of another era. His disheveled, gray hair reached down over wire rim glasses and almost tangled into his matching eyebrows. Joe tried to keep eye contact despite the ear and chest hair that seemed to be trying to escape from the poor guy. He wasn't all that different from the typical Midwest man.

"Eh, I don't know if you can. I've already been shot down a couple of times. Aren't you worried about *sleeping dogs*?" Joe said sarcastically.

"Listen, I'm a bit of an outsider, too. If you can come back around 7:00 p.m., we could talk. I know about your struggles, and I might be able to help," the stranger beckoned as he backed up and started to go. The gentleman looked like a local, but the way he talked assured Joe that he was indeed an outsider. He didn't tell Joe to "let sleeping dogs lie," and he spoke with an interesting confidence that intrigued Joe.

"All right, I guess," Joe mumbled as he watched the old guy shuffle out the door.

He was wearing the same shirt as the last time he came to the library. Joe dismissed him as an employee at the time because he made a couple of suggestions and knew his way around the place. To Joe, everyone in the library was a little strange. With the proliferation of the internet, most things could be found online, and most people didn't bother with analog research anymore. Many of us would probably admit the pitfalls of the new system but usually expressed the benefits outweighed the hazards.

But, especially to an author, sometimes it's simply good to physically touch the texts personally, even in a small town like this, and realize each one has a story behind it as well as the story in it. Even the damn history book of the county that, for some reason, left George Popper out and failed to include the one and only hotel. His frustration was starting to simmer a bit but at least someone was willing to help. He left the library about as quickly as he entered. He realized he would have to explain to Mary why he made the trip at all, being gone less than half an hour, but she might be excited for him that he had a promising lead.

Before he left, he stopped and interrupted the librarian still face-first in her book.

"What is that other guy's name that works here?" Joe asked politely.

"I'm the only one that works this shift ... budget cuts and all," she said, finally looking up.

"Well, then the guy that was here earlier ... the guy that just left."

"Oh, that's Jim ... Wait, maybe John ... Um, his name is definitely Bob!"

She quickly dove into her manual list of members at the library searching frantically for his membership card and name.

"You know, ever since I have worked here, I see him from time to time, and we always greet each other, but I can't honestly remember his name. I thought he had a library card, but I don't see one that matches up. He could be listed under the old system. I'll check into it."

"Not that big of a deal," Joe said, but he knew that it now was a big deal to her.

In a small town, knowing everyone's identity is a central part to the security of the small town. But Joe had enough mysteries running around in his mind, and he didn't care what the old man's name was or where he came from. He just wanted some answers, and this guy might be the opening he needed to crack this case wide open! It surprised him just a little that he was this serious, but his excitement about the mysterious man caused him to float home on a different arc than before.

THE MAN WITH
NO NAME

FOR THE THIRD TIME IN ONE DAY, HE UNAPOLOGETICALLY entered the library. He was 10 minutes early and didn't see anyone at the checkout desk. In a town this size, it was likely that she let this man watch the shop while she went home to eat supper. Joe quickly headed back to the genealogy room where he saw the older gentleman sitting perfectly in the old, hardwood chair. As Joe approached, the man held up one finger. Joe waited patiently as per the cue.

When he rested the book on the coffee table next to him, he raised, and both of them sort of bumped elbows like people were apt to do during the time of the virus. They both were wearing face masks, since the vaccine was probably a few months out for their area and the numbers were increasing. Joe noticed that the older fellow had a tough time keeping the mask up on his nose, and he made a joke to himself about keeping it up, but he decided not to say it out loud.

"I just love a great book," the man said.

Then he proceeded into a monologue about how stories are sacred and how it's a privilege to get to listen to someone else's relaying of what is important to them. Joe felt this somewhat as an author himself. The paperback novel that the older man was reading was around 80,000 words that the author had labored over for months, only to have others scrutinize and edit so that it was presentable to the public. Then, it was released which is somewhat like giving birth, Joe thought. To Joe, his attempt at writing a novel never made any money; but he remembered that his first book felt a little like sending his child off to college. It was traumatic in one way and triumphant in another.

"It's a shame, we don't read more," Joe thought out loud.

"Indeed," the older man confirmed. "But, more specifically I think we could read more stories. Some people think they are a waste of time. They even scoff at them like they're just chasing butterflies and wasting time when they could be doing something more productive. But stories are not a waste of time. Stories, even if they are fiction, are from the heart and soul of the author. They are a part of themselves that they shared with us. For me, it's an intimate thing. You're an author; you know what I mean. Don't you feel that way about your stories? "

"Well, I guess," Joe stammered. "Yes, I guess I do. Most of my stories are somewhat about myself, and I get emotional every time I read them. I want people to like them and enjoy them, and I think that's because I want them to delight in me as a person. Maybe, something like that!"

"I think it's exactly like that," his new friend said.

Joe listened to a couple more monologues before interrupting. He didn't like small talk, but it seemed like the old fellow had his number. He asked a lot of questions, but then he would tell a story about his life or give a bit of insight, and for whatever reason, Joe felt as though he had known the man forever. He didn't have a great relationship with his own father before his death, and this guy had the vibe of what Joe felt was important in a father figure.

"So ... You caught on that I was wondering about the hotel and the tunnels. What can you tell me?" Joe asked without any kind of transition ... he just dove right in as per his custom.

Unfortunately, the response was not quite as direct as the question. The older gentleman peered deep into his eyes, almost like he was searching for something inside of Joe. He wasn't struggling to remember the answer to what had been asked, it was more like he was trying to determine why it was being asked. Joe had fixed his impatient brow and felt his leg shake while he waited for the man to answer.

"Let me ask you this ... " he began.

Joe could feel himself getting tense. After arranging to meet, he had waited several additional hours making this the longest day in recent history. He was proud of himself for being present and not stressing, but what he was hoping for from this adventure was some concrete answers or some kind of definite plan to follow—a dried up drainage ditch, so to speak. The guy was charming, but he was about ready to have something he could write in his notebook to follow up on tomorrow. That was the plan he arranged in his mind—he wasn't prepared to answer questions.

" ... what exactly are you looking for?" the man continued. "Perhaps the townspeople don't know exactly what you are looking for, and they're just afraid to disappoint you. Can you say exactly what you are looking for or what you hope to find? What if someone came into your house and started poking around, and couldn't tell you exactly what they were looking for? How long would you let them stay? What would you ask them?"

"Most likely I would ask them exactly what they are looking for and what they intend to do with it when they find it." Joe answered proudly.

"Exactly, when you came into the library the other day, you knew exactly what you were looking for, and you asked for it. You were looking for the recorded history of the hotel, and the man that ran it for many years. You didn't know his name, but what you wanted was clear and you found it. But then, the treasure you sought wasn't exactly what you expected, and you got frustrated because now you don't know exactly what you are looking for, and that is a bit harder. It's also harder for people to help you because they can't read your mind. Is that a fair assessment?"

"Yeah, that is fair, I suppose."

Joe hung his head for a second and then stared at the older man. They just stared at each other for a few seconds. He assumed he was perfectly ready for this adventure, but he didn't prepare for the bumps in the road that are normal for most journeys. He wanted the answers to come quickly and the treasures to be spectacular. From the older man, he was hoping for the secret key that unlocked all the other mysteries in the town.

"It's easy to judge other people, isn't it?"

"Yeah, I suppose it is," Joe admitted.

"I would love to help you, but I think you need to take a step back and figure out what it is exactly that you hope to find. What exactly are you looking for?"

There were about a dozen things Joe wanted to say, but he held back. This was all too familiar to him. He would imagine a journey, then plow through some bumpy parts, only to be stymied because of miscalculations and unexpected challenges. Setting goals, working hard, and achieving things was easy for Joe, but the real adventures into the unknown always came to this place where he realized it was going to be harder than he imagined. In addition, he would probably have to ask someone for help and that meant he wasn't going to be able to do it on his own.

He groaned inwardly to himself, but outwardly he simply responded, "Okay."

They nodded to each other and just looked at each other for a few seconds before they stood simultaneously and shuffled around trying to figure out how to close this chapter.

"I'll think about that and get back to you," Joe said.

"That sounds promising! I'm looking forward to it!"

As he was walking toward the door, he turned and asked, "By the way, what is your name?"

"It's George," the old man said with a kind of half salute, half wave.

Joe didn't even stop to consider the irony or the fact that he didn't know how to contact George. He was too busy thinking about the question asked, and he slipped into his car and drove the short distance back to his house. He knew that the excitement of the tunnels, and thoughts of gangsters and church history had derailed him from the initial journey.

What am I looking for? he thought to himself over and over. He didn't remember falling asleep that night, only the question. He had thoughts of the Oak Island television show he and his wife enjoyed and about how people had been interested in the show for years. But, on that show, they know what they are looking for, sort of. Joe knew in his heart that the tunnels weren't what he was looking for although he was sure they were down there somewhere, and possibly, they were connected.

He just needed some time to think. Another look? No, first just some time to think.

WALLS, WALLS, WALLS

EARLY THE NEXT MORNING, JOE MESSAGED MARLA ABOUT the parts of the hotel building that they hadn't explored. There was a first-floor area (the big ballroom) that was closed off for some reason and the basement below that (where the mysterious car was supposedly located). In the basement, he remembered there being a solid wall with no evident doorway. There were a couple of doorways on the first floor, but Marla told him it was closed to the public.

A quick text message to Marla cleared up some confusion. She told him that her husband keeps his tools on the 1st floor and didn't want the public in that area. He thought about asking to see it, but he didn't want to be too pushy this early on. She gave the impression that there is just no way to get into the basement from there!

They talked about where information had originated, which by the way is an appropriate thing to say when someone tells you some gossip or hearsay (Where did you get that information?). It was at that time that she mentioned Aaron who owned a local business.

"His family has been around for a long time, and he knows a lot about these things," Marla offered.

For the moment, that was enough for Joe. Another lead that might be more cooperative was just what he needed. But the visit with George had softened him a bit. He took some time this morning just to sit and think for a while. He knew Aaron from the time he was a deacon, and he would contact him later when the rest of the world was awake. To be proactive, he decided to go ahead and leave a message, but Aaron answered the phone.

Aaron couldn't remember a lot but he thought his mom might have some pictures. He also knew several historians in the area and gave those names to Joe. Joe resolved to call them all after lunch. For now, he just wanted to write a little and realign.

After the meeting with George, he had immediately felt exposed and a little defensive as one who was told the truth. But the candor of the old fellow was just what he needed though not necessarily what he wanted. Why had he gotten so angry at the townsfolk? Why was this treasure hunt becoming the most important thing in his life? And why did everything feel like a wall?

From his work with people over the years and his own internal struggles, he knew this was about far more than old campfire stories about a man and his hotel. Joe was suspicious of the things inside him that he couldn't see, but he knew that they were there anyway. He saw the correlation but had no idea how to get through the walls of his own subconscious. He was hoping for a miraculous revelation, but something in him told him he would have to wait for answers, and that this was a wall he couldn't knock down. There might be a way in, but it was going to take time and patience and for now, he needed to be still.

Over the years, Joe had learned to be grateful. In times of deep desperation, he was often subtly reminded to be grateful for what was instead of making the next quest the only thing that counted. He also knew that religion could misuse this concept to bypass important things and dismiss what is pressing and difficult. This type of gratitude he only found when he was still. As Mary left for work, he unexpectedly told her, "I'm glad I'm married to you."

This kind of gratefulness comes from deep inside, and he surprised himself and Mary when he blurted it out. He supposed that it also had something to do with compassion because, suddenly, he was even grateful for the people that were reluctant to share information, and were just trying to protect what they valued. Very soon, Joe would be back on the investigative trail, but for now, what was most important was to be quiet and to be grateful.

In these quiet times, when humility caused him to pause, Joe also felt a deep sense of unity with other people. His mom was a benefit-of-the-doubt type of person, but Joe noticed that people took advantage of this. So, he was a little more cautious and tended to be a little more judgmental. When he was quiet, he often realized that, essentially, we are all in the same boat. We all juggle things like judgment, fear, and anxiety. Yet, dealing with these issues in the heat of the moment is never effective, he reasoned. We never resolve them when we are reacting to the stupid things that people like David might be apt to do at any given moment.

But, more than anything, he thought about his motivation. Why did he need to know about this old hotel? Why was it important to get the facts? Why did it matter about secrets that a town keeps? Subconsciously, he knew that it was about something inside himself, and he reasoned that if he found some answers about the hotel, then he would see the correlations inside his own person.

In his five decades on earth, he had at least discovered several things that were not the answer. He knew that religion was not the answer for him. He had a deep suspicion that whatever holds deep power over us doesn't usually magically disappear. There must be some deep introspection and a bit of hard work. He also knew that ignoring anything didn't make it go away. In fact, it just came back in a slightly different package later—usually more intense and harder to manage. He was also beginning to realize that we are human *beings* and not human *doings* and sometimes the best thing we can do is just be present.

Joe was attempting to just be still and present when he got distracted. So, he picked up his phone and started to play a video game. It was ironic because it was a tank game, and his stances on war, and such, had become a lot more anti-violence. But, for the moment, it distracted him enough to not go and DO something until later in the day when he was sure that his head was on straight. He realized that he was distracting himself from being distracted and just chuckled to himself a little at the contradiction. Before he knew it, he was knee-deep in earning a new tank with all the features for his courageous work on the battlefield of his phone.

JULY 1914 — NEAR THE RIVER

THE TWO YOUNG MEN LAID FOOT-TO-FOOT EXHAUSTED from their skirmish. World War I was just getting into full swing and tensions were high on all fronts. A spirited wrestling or boxing match was just enough of a distraction and just enough of a test of manhood to keep men that *could have been serving* distracted from the guilt and shame they might otherwise have felt.

George Popper had served in the army for four years before being released honorably just a few months before. As he heaved from exhaustion, his muscles rippled in the dim sunlight and sweat poured from his body. Red welts and abrasions were appearing, but as he felt around, nothing was strained or broken. The other guy, a wiry sort who most people called Zork, was mostly okay except his nose was bleeding, and he limped a little when he tried to get up. They both sat exhausted for a few minutes to regain composure.

Then, almost like it was a cue, they both stared at each other and started to laugh. They stood in unison and shook hands, followed by an embrace. Struck by the moment, they couldn't form very coherent words, but their body language acquiesced that the fight would end in a draw. George, the largest of the contestants, was the final match, and Zork was the only one brave enough to take him on. The others fumbled around trying to separate their money, wondering how to handle a draw. Someone was supposed to win.

Alesa had left earlier because she couldn't watch her favorite guy get hurt. She had signaled her departure; George had acknowledged and turned to face his opponent. They had always enjoyed that type of closeness. The couple were friends in high school, and after a brief summer romance (the first for both of them), they decided it wasn't the right time for a serious romance. He went to the army, and she started helping at her uncle's hotel downtown.

It was a couple of years later when they began writing and just never stopped growing closer until George returned home on a technicality, and they were soon married. Neither family objected because most of them were rooting for this union all along.

George was working with his father on the farm and Alesa always juggled several projects at once. She would resolve problems at the hotel, then work on a community project or Christmas gifts or whatever piqued her interest. She was the right kind of busybody and George was just the opposite. He liked to plan and strategize about the farm and discover or invent new innovative strategies to be more efficient. Occasionally, he would go hunting or buy a new gun, but mostly he was saving and planning for a better life for the two of them. He was quiet; she was not. And on and on it went. These two opposites were infatuated with each other.

Arriving home to their modest place just outside town, he made a beeline for the shower and didn't even bother putting his clothes back on. He knew where he was headed, and the towel was enough for him. The years of being in the army had overcome his modesty about his body. In addition, he was in perfect shape and didn't have anything to hide. Alesa met him in the kitchen and almost caught her breath before he lifted her high and then gently lowered her back down close to himself.

They kissed deeply like newlyweds do except the vibration they felt was something that had grown over time. Their maturity and sincerity deepened their respect and love for each other. But for now, there was passion.

Neither one of them remembered much of the flurry of activity that took place before they collapsed onto their bed. It was the middle of the afternoon, but it was Saturday, so they laid next to each other talking about the wrestling match and all the other things that happened that day.

They decided to eat dinner in town which was a luxury saved for this once-a-week occasion. There weren't many options, but they always went to the restaurant also owned by her uncle. A battle with the owner over who paid the bill usually ended in a free meal for the Poppers, so they didn't abuse the hospitality and only came in once a week and sometimes, for Sunday brunch.

After the meal, they walked down to the yet-to-be-named Memorial Building. It was a community gathering place for all types of activities. They sat on the steps and kissed a little, but mostly just sat and watched people walk by, occasionally gazing up at the stars.

That night, Alesa could tell that something was troubling her husband. She was more likely to talk, and if she became angry, she was a force to be reckoned with. Even in the wrestling match, George was subdued and was given to thinking about things for extended periods of time before talking about them. But she could tell that something was bubbling up in him just like the day he proposed. She sensed this was something big, so she readied herself and inquired.

"What is it, Babe?"

"I've just been thinking about something," he answered.

"No kidding," she said, and realized too late that she had vocalized her thoughts.

He wasn't startled by her directness because he knew her mannerisms well, and he was confident about himself, even though he restlessly searched for the words to say. He scratched the dirt with his nice shoes and fiddled with the bottom of his untucked shirt.

"Come on, just spit it out," she said. "I can take it."

"I want us to look into taking over the hotel. Your uncle is frustrated with the place, and I have so many ideas to make it better. So many people drive by here and with a few modifications, this could be the biggest thing to happen to the area. We're saving money well, and it shouldn't take long to wrestle up a down payment. This could be our thing!"

He laughed, realizing he said *wrestle* after the events of the day.

"But, what about us raising a family?" she offered. "Ya know, we haven't even talked about that. We're just getting started, having fun … Could we still have a Saturday afternoon love fest if we ran the hotel? I'm not at all negative, it's just one of those things we should think through, right?"

"Absolutely, but what a better way to raise a family than to involve them in the family business. I think you and I could do this! We don't have to know all the details up front. It might be like a destiny thing—like we're supposed to do it! You have so much experience there, and I have so many ideas. This could be great!"

To be honest, Alesa had never heard this type of emotion in his voice. He was usually subdued and matter of fact. He took the "Let your yes be 'yes' and your no be 'no'" advice seriously. She also knew George's dad was content to farm and hunt, but George had a different kind of restlessness in him that required more from life. The army had awakened the desire in him. He saw various places and diverse cultures, but he also realized the people that succeeded out there weren't much different from him. Combine this with his physical stature, and he genuinely wasn't afraid of anything—at least not yet.

They talked a little on the way home and then for a couple of hours more. Eventually, they found themselves ready for bed. When he drew Alesa close, he could tell they were gearing up for round two. But then they both paused, and she glared at him like something mattered that she was about to say.

"Okay, let's do it! Let's run a damn hotel! I'm in!"

This would be the first of many times they would look in each other's eyes and commit to a new venture, but every time it was like this. They agreed to move forward together. They forgot about the hotel for the rest of the night, but both woke up dreaming about the possibilities.

It didn't happen overnight. After seven hard-working years, they stood in the street as owners and operators of Hotel Popper.

MARCH 1921 — HOTEL POPPER AND THE ROARING 20s

THERE WERE MANY CHALLENGES ABOUT LIVING IN A small town, but this was one of the better things. Refreshments were spread out in the small lobby, but guests and community members spilled out on the porch and into the streets. Times like these were more about reunions and conversation, but as the fresh coat of paint on the front of the hotel indicated, this was the start of something new.

Small towns are always excited when the younger people stay and help out with the development of the town. George and Alesa were two of their favorites. This was truly an exciting time for everyone involved.

The 1920s were a time of prosperity in the United States and mass consumerism. People wanted to spend their money. George knew this because he was well-read and thought a lot about how to make their business appealing. During the first year, he mainly just expanded the dining and the dance floor. Guests wanted to eat out and have fun at the same time. For many years after, the place was packed every night so that they had to turn people away at the doors.

George and Alesa would stand back occasionally and just watch the money flow into the hotel before something needed their attention, and they would dart off to take care of it. The couple were exhausted every night, but George still made time to help his father farm and occasionally worked the night shift at the hotel. They inhabited the apartment on the bottom floor of the hotel that lay just beyond the lobby, but they took occasional days off to retreat to their own house, while various relatives filled in.

They felt like the luckiest people alive, until one day they talked about starting a family. Upon further examination, George found out that he had an issue that couldn't be fixed, and those dreams were put on hold. Alesa cried for several days, and George just appeared deep in thought. They took the weekend off and went fishing at the home place where they were sure no one would find them. After a day of silent fishing, Alesa was the first to speak.

"You know having children has actually never been one of my goals," she said reluctantly.

"Really?" George questioned, as he gazed up from untangling a fishing line.

"It's just what is usually expected, but I have never personally wanted it very much. This wave we are on is worth riding. We're saving so much money and enjoying success. Our guests act like we're family probably because we treat them the same way. This is an experience I don't want to miss because I'm all wrapped up in motherhood. Does that sound selfish?"

"If it does, then I am selfish, too," he said. "I enjoy the life we have, and I can't wait to see what comes next. I'm sure there will be challenges, but for now it is about as wonderful as I can imagine."

They settled the matter and then took advantage of their remote location. They made love there on the dock. The experience turned out to be less than what either of them imagined, and they vowed to make it up to each other when they got back to the house.

The following year, George invested with another community member and started a gun shop right next to the hotel. His friend from high school was struggling to make ends meet but had tremendous knowledge and skill with munitions. Part of the influx of capital to the town was that people from bigger cities wanted to come to flyways nearby and hunt various migratory waterfowl. The area was rich with deer and turkey and other wild game. The gun shop was just another piece in the puzzle for people getting away to spend their money and escape the city.

Part of the allure was that they were always present. Even though they were only in their early 30s, they were always more like mom and dad to most people that came through. George would stand and watch when young adults and children would wander up from other parts of town to get a bite to eat before making sure they got back to where they should be before the wilder crowd came out to play.

Oh, the wilder crowd! It was common for George to get a proposal from a drunk flapper from the city nearly every night, but he would always just point to Alesa at the counter. She was so beautiful and her look so intense that the girls knew to back off from her man. The couple's routine kept them honest. They didn't ever long to be somewhere else. This was their dream, and it was only getting better. They didn't have time to go on vacation because they were too busy living in the place that other people came to get away. They understood this early, and it helped them keep perspective.

Prohibition didn't hit the small towns like it did in urban areas, but George prepared for it just the same. Early in the life of the hotel, he began a secret project to build a wine cellar. He wanted it to be a secret, so he only involved his business partner, his lovely wife, and a couple of family members. Alcohol was also a normal ingredient of their life and the times, even though some acted like they didn't even know it was there. Perhaps that was why the secret was kept for so long.

"We can always keep things a secret here," George bellowed one day, "because a lot of people don't want to admit that certain things exist and although they don't admit they exist, they are too proper to step foot near it, so it will always survive. Something like that!"

He might have been a bit tipsy at the time. He never drank during normal business hours, but sometimes had a couple of extra ones at night to help quiet his mind and put himself to sleep.

When the first government inspector arrived to investigate alcohol sales, George was already a step ahead of them and had most of the evidence hidden away in the basement. The next night they served alcohol freely but never kept too much in plain sight. It was a system that worked extremely well and never drew too much attention. It made him feel a little guilty to skirt the law, but he just never agreed with the premise of it and did his best to keep everything kind of sensible.

The basement area that they dug out was about half the size of the hotel. It abutted their own basement but extended out to the North via a secret door wide enough to move kegs and other large deliveries that came to the back after they closed at night. A family member made sure everything was discrete and locked up before cleaning the rest of the downstairs and that everything was perfect for the morning.

So many circumstances and situations worked out for the couple. That was, until some of them didn't.

The depression that came in '29 was challenging to everyone and eventually the smallest of towns and the best of people.

SEPTEMBER 1925 — THE VISITOR

HE APPEARED OUT OF NOWHERE. ALTHOUGH THE GUESTS of the hotel were varied and diverse, this man stood out. His expertly tailored suit and neat hair cut identified him as someone associated with wealth. George was able to identify his suit as Italian from his travels overseas even though he still had on his overalls from earlier that day. The man's eyes darted around briefly and proceeded directly to inquire with George who was standing next to the desk talking to Alesa.

"May I speak with the owner?" he said politely.

"You are speaking with the owners," George said, smiling proudly and without apology.

It was a common mistake. Although George stood out from the crowd, he didn't bother to spend any time on physical appearance except that he learned from the Army to stay well-shaven and get haircuts from Alesa on a regular basis. Even if he had the time to buy a fancy suit, nothing in him wanted to do anything like that. But there was no mistaking that this was a person that had access to such things.

"Hello, my name is Conrad Daniels."

"George and Alesa Popper."

"Nice to meet you. This is a gem of a place. We've heard prolific things in the city about this establishment, and I'm pleasantly surprised. We were here a while back, and you have made amazing progress."

"Thank you so much," Alesa chimed in. "This is our home, and everyone that comes through here is family."

Conrad peered deep into her eyes and then began to nod his head in agreement. It scared her a little, but it was almost like he was evaluating them and that was likely what he was paid to do—assess situations and people for whomever he worked for. George thought to himself, as he often did, sometimes silence speaks louder than words.

"Can we possibly arrange a spot where our associates could conduct a meeting?" Conrad said. "Some of them are coming from different directions, and this is a perfect spot to meet. I know it's short notice, but perhaps this will help."

Conrad counted off five $20 bills and handed them to George. The couple had long since gotten over being shy about taking gratuities. People often were just appreciative that their needs were met and wanted to share their abundance. Most often, they would gather up that money at the end of the day and share about half of it with the staff. The other half went in a coffee can. The can was tucked way back in the back of the counter, almost impossible to spot. Occasionally a young person would need something, and the couple made it a practice to give generously when there was a legitimate need. Despite this generosity, the can was always full, and they even occasionally exchanged some smaller bills for larger ones.

"Well, we don't have a meeting room," George began, "but I've been working on a little project. Come with me, and we'll see what we can do."

He led them back to what was originally just the empty space in the middle of the back part of the hotel's first floor. George had been finishing the walls and smoothing out the floors in hopes of one day having a ballroom or an event space. Conrad surveyed the room quickly and was not impressed, but George was determined to find a solution.

"I know it's not fancy, but it's big enough for a private meeting."

His eyes lit up as George explained that they could drag a few tables in and cover them.

"Whatever you need," George promised. "We'll make it happen."

"Okay, we will need a dedicated server for dinner. Then later, we will need them to let us alone for the meeting, which shouldn't take long. And someone to serve drinks later. What we mainly need is someone to make sure we can have a private meeting and attend to our not-that-elaborate needs for a couple of hours. Oh, and we'll also need a few rooms in case some of us drink a little too much after the meeting."

Alesa stared down nervously at the register. It was getting later in the afternoon, and it was customary for them to be booked most nights. She almost rose in disappointment, but then she remembered a couple of cancellations.

"We have exactly three rooms!" she said, relieved.

"Good, we'll take the rooms and trust that you'll attend to all the arrangements."

"We absolutely will," Alesa offered.

With that, Conrad scurried out the front door. They glanced at each other for a minute or so, and then both just quietly went to work. This felt like something important. The $100 was enough to secure the reservation, and Conrad didn't appear to be a person that took too many "no's." He was kind and courteous, but he was also professional.

"We didn't even get a name," Alesa said to herself.

About that time, Conrad reappeared in the front door.

"J.D. Enterprises, that's the name! For the bill! Thanks, friends," he said warmly and, for the first time, smiled a bit before disappearing again.

The rest of the day was normal. They almost forgot about Conrad and the unusual circumstances after the arrangements were made. The restaurant was packed, the dance floor bustling, the hotel near capacity. There was so much to do that the busy couple was startled to see him reappear at the entrance. Somehow, with the older crowd and a few other business guests, he didn't stand out as much as earlier in the day.

"This is outstanding! This will work fine!" Conrad seemed a little too excited as he patted George on the back and gave Alesa a hug. "My deepest gratitude," he continued as he rolled off another hundred or so from his front pocket stash.

"No," Alesa started to protest, but he was already off inspecting and assessing everything whispering to himself.

They decided to leave him alone, but soon other businessmen started to arrive. About the time Alesa would offer help, each would catch Conrad's eye from the back, nod to Alesa, and proceed back to the makeshift meeting room. Alesa decided to have Nancy Plemmons run the front desk. She had been training to do this for months and as the co-owner of the hotel, Alesa wanted to make sure everything went right.

Straightening and adjusting herself in the mirror, Alesa hurried back to the room and took a slight step back when she discovered there were already over a dozen men in suits greeting each other. She must have been in a daze because she hadn't noticed that many people came through the front door. Eventually they noticed her, and all silenced.

"Hello, I'm Alesa, my husband George and I want to welcome you to Hotel Popper. I will be your server. Please let me know if you need anything this evening. We are at your service, and we hope you feel at home here. If you are here, you are family!"

A smile came across most of their faces except for the few like Conrad that were busy arranging and sorting papers. They all acknowledged Alesa warmly and grunted their thanks at various tones. She felt appreciated, unlike the looks she often got from men scanning her features. Every one of them met her eyes and then waited for her to speak again.

"Can I get you some drinks or an appetizer?" It just came out of habit from helping in the restaurant.

"Alesa, why don't you just bring us a couple of bottles of your best wine and some menus," Conrad began. "These jackasses will have you running all over the place. Don't let them take advantage. Just keep the wine flowing, and they will be fine."

Alesa smiled at his directness, even though something told her most of these men didn't take much crap from anyone. They were playful with Conrad, like George was with his brother, but she took a deep breath when she realized that the men were probably not like anyone she had met before. Briefly she felt like a little girl, or some-one else in a different time, but quickly she came back to reality and started anticipating needs and making the arrangements.

Almost immediately, George appeared from downstairs with some wine in a wooden box. Alesa didn't know if he had been listening or instinctively knew, but they quickly were rallying whoever they could find to quickly chill the wine and locate a few snacks to keep the new guests happy. George loved learning about wines and sharing that knowledge with others although something told him these guests would be way ahead of the curve.

George had also slipped into the apartment and put on a casual jacket, ditched the overalls, and straightened himself a little. His stint in the military helped him appreciate appropriate dress and the nature of situations a little better, but he would probably always be a little rough around the edges and somewhat rebellious.

"My husband has selected a wine to get you started and with your permission, we would like to serve you the chef's favorite dish, Chicken Parmesan," Alesa announced.

"That's perfect," Conrad interrupted before anyone could say any-thing else.

His determination to keep order and not having to wrestle through everyone's preferences was a small step in the right direction. Alesa was getting better over the years at empathically knowing what her guests wanted which only made her customer service even more impeccable, especially for a little town. She was about to inform the chef, when J.D. walked in, and all the other men fell silent.

She wasn't sure how these men just appeared out of nowhere, but it was the same with the boss. He was about the same size as George, but his dress and demeanor were different. His confidence seemed to flow out of him like a fog. He was dressed impeccably. His face was hard as a rock, but his eyes were soft and compassionate. He almost teared up when he saw the men, but he turned to Conrad for the introduction.

"Alesa, this is Jon, but most people call him J.D. Alesa and George own the hotel and all the accouterments that surround it."

Several of the men started to chuckle at Conrad's attempt at fancy words, but they were silenced quickly with a look from this new man who was obviously feared. Everything about him commanded respect and someone randomly handed him a glass of wine before he even asked, and another took his coat without ceremony. There was a dance playing out that didn't need words. Apparently, they had all been together before, and they knew their roles.

"So, nice to meet you Alesa," J.D. said as he stretched out his arms to embrace her warmly.

She wondered how George would handle all the hugs. He wasn't a physical person with anyone other than his wife, and most of his family followed suit. Alesa's family was just the opposite, and she had experienced all kinds of people in the years so far at the hotel. She had come to realize hugs can mean different things at different times. Some people hug because they are needy. Some people use them as a vehicle to accomplish something else. But there is a hug that comes from a family member, and that is what this hug felt like. She took a second to absorb it, and then she stepped back and smiled.

"Make yourself at home, sir. If you need anything, I will be over there."

Alesa positioned herself where she could see the restaurant with one eye and the back room of men with the other. She didn't want anything to go wrong with this new family, and she only stepped out of her lookout spot occasionally to check on details. George was absorbed in his wine service delivery, and the customers were pleased with all his selections. He kept disappearing into the basement, only to return with more options. Since everyone was happy, Alesa left it alone.

It was almost an hour before the chef arrived to announce his creation and the limited options for substitutions. The men were satisfied, and they went right back to discussing other things. The chef paused like he was waiting for something, so Conrad again spoke up.

"Why don't you just take the vegetable options and put them in some large bowls."

"Great idea," the chef quickly agreed and darted off into the kitchen.

It was a grand thing to have a chef in a small town during those times. Ricky had gone to the finest schools and learned from the best, but after his wife died, he didn't have any motivation to live in Manhattan and returned home where he could simply focus on making people happy. On any given day, he would be just as busy making burgers and fries as he was later preparing roasted duck for a demanding guest. He was pleased to be on either end of the spectrum. The couple appreciated their luck in having him onboard, and they often remembered to tell him so.

Alesa was reveling in the fact that she was ahead of almost every request the men had. They were less demanding than the regular crowd, at least that is how she interpreted it. On one hand, she understood that the less you have the more you try to squeeze out of every dollar you spend, and she remembered the days when she and George could only eat here once a week. On the other hand, she hoped that people could relax and enjoy each other's company like the men in the back room. Sometimes money can become an obstacle, and other times it can take away the pressure to allow everyone to simply gather and be themselves.

"Alesa, can you help us?" Conrad queried from the back room.

Her mind had begun to wonder, so Conrad's request startled her back to the present. She was trying her best to take all this in. She was only slightly embarrassed because everything was running like clockwork.

"We're going to begin the meeting if you will leave us for about a half hour … I'll let you know."

"Absolutely, I'll get the doors," she said as something relaxed; only then did she realize how tense she had become.

That tension remained most of the night. It was that part of her that wanted to do well. Her father was overly critical, and her mom and siblings responded with unquestioned obedience. It wasn't like the respect that J.D. demanded from his *associates*, but she sensed it was somehow related. Most of the time, she didn't let it influence her in the present and could keep it subdued; however, when she became frustrated, it was almost like trying to keep a beach ball submerged under water. When that happened, she would erupt into almost a fit of rage to bring situations back under control. The staff knew that this would happen once or twice a year, and they didn't take it personally.

She took a seat and nearly fell asleep. George's fingers rubbed between her shoulder blades both stimulating and relaxing her. She loved how much she loved him, and the way he respected her. Oddly enough, that is what she appreciated the most from J.D.—he respected her. But sadly, she regretted the times when she lost emotional control, respect was what she was least able to show to others. More than money or vacations or anything else, she longed to find the underlying cause of this flaw in her otherwise delightful character.

"Ricky is preparing a special dessert for them. I tasted it. You won't believe it!" George softly whispered, intentionally brushing up against her neck seductively.

"You better stop. You're fast, but we don't have time for that," she snapped with a grin.

They both realized about the same time that Nancy probably could hear what they were saying, and they flushed a little with embarrassment. A friend of the family, recently widowed, she was capable and fun to be around. She was plain-looking in most ways, but her well-kept appearance attracted people to her. She was going to make a capable host for the front desk once she learned everything that Alesa could teach her. She had handled everything well tonight, and they all just chuckled together about the embarrassing incident.

"You know most of them tipped me for taking their coats? I made more from tips than you guys paid me tonight," Nancy smiled as she popped her head into the hall.

"That's great, Nancy. We like our new guests," Alesa answered.

"Is there anything else you need before I check out in about 15 minutes?"

"No, we should be fine from here on out. Most of the guests are checked in. The restaurant is dying down, and the night crowd probably will be slower than usual because of that thing across the river. Is it a rodeo? I don't even know. Someone needs to make a calendar of all those things."

"Oh, you should know the busybodies are on a rotation. I think they want to know what's going on?"

They both laughed. There were about a dozen women around town that felt a deep need to know everything. Alesa has seen a group of them enter through the hotel and strain their necks toward the backroom before slowly making their way to the restaurant. Nancy entertained an unusual number of bogus questions as various ones of them peered over her shoulder to get a better assessment of the situation. The couple's strict policy about guest anonymity held up, and so most of the townspeople knew not even to ask. Alesa once told the gossiper's unofficial leader, "If they want you to know who they are, they will tell you."

"Ha, there's a couple of them still in the restaurant," Alesa offered.

Just about that time, she heard George teasing the women about being drunk and that was probably the reason for them being out so late. Of course, they drank, but these were the type of people that wouldn't admit it for various reasons, and so all they could do was gasp a little at the insinuation and hastily make up a phony excuse. George chuckled to himself, trying to be polite to the women, and disappeared back into his workshop. He knew them all too well and that their intentions were good—it was just one of the few things that frustrated him.

"We're all done," Conrad said, breaking in. "Sorry we went a little long."

"We have some desert if you want!" Alesa offered.

Most of the men in the meeting took a bathroom break, and others went out on the porch to smoke a cigar and sip the brandy George had somehow slipped into the meeting. The busy bodies were leaving and took a calculated assessment of the men on the porch. They felt startled when the men greeted them, and they scurried off into the night. The men just smiled among themselves.

"Oh man, I wouldn't have to have sex with my wife if I had this desert at home," the wiry associate offered up while others just moaned and smiled at his comment. J.D. shot him another look, and he decided not to pursue his observation any further.

"Anything else I can get you?" Alesa asked.

"Nah," Conrad concluded, "A few of us will turn in for the night. Some of us must hit the road. We might talk for a while, but we have everything we need."

"Okay, we'll be turning in soon," George reminded them. "The night shift is in. Just knock on our door if you need anything."

Even with the excitement, the couple fell asleep almost instantly. Alesa laughed because she could tell that George had sampled all the alcohol that he had brought to the guests. She was content because virtually everything went smoothly and that was what mattered most to her. She had performed well. The staff worked together and as she reached down and felt her pockets, she remembered they also made a lot of money tonight.

When George awoke later to go to the bathroom, he realized that the hotel was dark except for a small light in the newly ordained ball-room/conference room. There was a candle on the table, remnant from a past celebration and not that uncommon to remove smells like cigar smoke. He almost didn't notice him sitting there, but as he emerged from the restroom and headed back to his warm and toasty bed, he caught the shadow of a lone man staring at something. He wasn't positive, but it appeared to be J.D. still seated at the table.

"You okay, man?" George said sheepishly.

J.D. didn't respond. He just raised up and tried to sniff away the tears and shook his head no.

THE CONVERSATION

GEORGE HAD NEVER SEEN HIS FATHER, WHOM EVERYONE called "Bud," show much emotion. During George's first 18 years of life, his father generally worked to the point of exhaustion building the farm. When he came home to rest and eat, there was little energy for anything except the bare requirements for family interaction. George did feel loved by his mother, but both of his parents were children of immigrants, and their best hope was to build something for their offspring.

When there was nothing to do, his parents didn't feel comfortable resting. So, anything like a "snow day" that should have been fun didn't turn out well for George and often ended traumatically. Even when incidents didn't directly involve him, he was held responsible—because he was the oldest. The Army helped him gain some new perspectives, but also introduced him to new trauma. He was at least able to forgive his dad, but he didn't respect him or feel close to him.

J.D. was a father figure and about 20 years his senior, but he was opposite to his dad. This man was much more open with his affection and emotions. The object of his sadness lay on the table in front of him, and George was beginning to piece together the situation as he sat across from the broken man. The picture revealed one of the most beautiful women that George had ever seen.

She was in her thirties, dark hair, deep brown eyes. Beyond that, it was hard to describe what he saw. The woman had movie star good looks, but she also had a toughness similar to J.D. He couldn't have described her if someone asked, but George might have remarked that she was incredibly striking. He wasn't embarrassed like when he occasionally saw a picture of a naked woman. It was more like respect. He realized he had stared at the picture too long and gazed up.

"She's beautiful," he said directly into J.D.'s eyes.

At first J.D. only nodded. Then he began to speak.

"Your wife actually got me going with her hug today. Sofia used to hug me like that. She was the most loving, genuine person on the planet, and, in a way, she taught me how to love. I am in no way a perfect man, but she treated me like it was impossible not to love me. I realized today how much I miss her, and a little wine loosened me up enough to feel what I'm feeling. This cry has been coming for a long time, and I appreciate the fact that I had a nice comfortable setting to let this out. It feels freeing to let your emotions out, know what I mean?"

"Not really," George said. "I've never been that good at emotions. Tell me more about your Sofia."

"Both of our parents were immigrants from Italy, and our families were all extremely close. We grew up together, and I never wanted anyone else except her. She was the object of my desire from the very moment I started desiring women. She was occasionally disappointed in me, but her love for me was constant. Our families all showed emotion, but her care for me was legendary. She was the strongest of women, but she used her strength to care for everyone, especially me."

"I feel much the same way about Alesa, she loves me in a way that no one else can," George offered.

"I see that," J.D. continued. "It's obvious that you are the apple of her eye, but she also has energy for every person she meets. Something is driving her, and it is almost like she redirects that into passion for everything she does. I think you are a lucky man!"

"Indeed, I am," George responded, a little surprised that this relative stranger knew so much about Alesa in just an evening of brief encounters.

The men stared at each other for several minutes as though empathically connected. It was new to George to see true feelings and not have to guess what was behind the stare. He saw what J.D. was feeling, because it was obvious. The older man knew that George was stuck because of whatever happened in his past. J.D. also knew that he couldn't change his new, younger friend at this moment. There was no magic advice, no quick fixes—only hard work and time heals wounds. He was surprised that he let George see so much of him, but he hoped it would be beneficial for both of them, eventually.

The men stood simultaneously and embraced realizing it was the end of a long day and more.

"If you close the doors, I'll sleep on that couch over there. I've got what I need. I'll see you tomorrow."

George started to object, but he knew the entire place was packed with people. He found a "Do Not Disturb Sign" to put on the doors and blew out the candle that was straining to stay lit. He surprised himself by touching J.D.'s shoulder with a quick grip and a caring look. He wondered how he could have feelings for someone he had just met only a few hours ago. He didn't sleep the rest of the night. Instead, he pondered the events of the day.

Inevitably, his mind ventured back to the incident that happened over 20 years prior. His father had suffered some setbacks on the farm. Weather and economic conditions had made everything tough for the struggling family. Everyone had to pitch in and even though George was only 12 or 13, he spent most of his free time laboring like a full-grown man. One afternoon, he and his brothers took some liberty and ventured less than a mile from the house—to the edge of town where all kinds of magical things happened.

It most likely took them more than a half-hour to reach town because they were exploring everything along the way. Every discovery led them to another adventure—it was just a natural progression to see and feel as many things as possible on their only night of freedom.

They chased a possum only long enough to discover something rotten that they couldn't identify. The brothers gagged and coughed and then started to jog as they got closer to the edge of town. They paused briefly behind the bank before cautiously proceeding to this land of excitement.

They quickly decided to sneak around town stealing mostly food items and admiring the people that came out mostly at night to celebrate a little. They created a game—find a drunk person wandering around, steal their hat, and hide it behind the town jail. They had accumulated about 10 hats from various townsfolk before some residents started to get wise that something was going on. With every minute that passed, more eyes were watching, and their game got tougher and tougher.

His younger brother, Nate had a brilliant idea.

"Let's moon 'em! They're all up there at the saloon. We'll just run out in the street and get 'em good! Those old, drunk bastards will never catch us!"

They were on a high from the hat stealin', and it was easy to branch out into a different brand of foolery—a natural progression. They were blowing off steam, and they found themselves directly in front of the saloon, trembling with excitement.

"Okay, on the count of three." They couldn't stop laughing.

Several people were beginning to peer out of various windows and doors to see what was happening in the middle of the street. The boys were still laughing and even stumbling, imitating the drunks they saw earlier that night. Eventually, they were able to compose themselves enough to turn in unison and face away from the crowd.

"Hey, are you the little creeps that are stealing people's hats? Hey, those are the Popper kids!"

"One, two, three," they whispered softly as they dropped their pants and then immediately began to run.

They couldn't hear the crowd because the adrenaline was so intense that it sounded more like a drum beat than actual sounds in their ears. They ran hard and fast down the length of main street. They turned around to see the crowd agitated but not in pursuit as they rounded the corner towards home. They didn't see the wagon hitched to their mule Betsy until they crashed into it and fell to the ground.

George felt a strong grip on his overall straps shortly before he was lifted into the back of the wagon followed by his two younger siblings. His father couldn't even talk; he was just mumbling to himself as he coaxed the mule into action and headed home. The boys considered celebrating their escape but thought better of it and just stared blankly at each other with wide eyes and sunken faces. The ride home was quick and direct. The siblings didn't want to be at home, and they didn't want to be in town—they were hoping they could disappear.

When the wagon came to a stop in front of their home, none of them moved. George felt the familiar grasp on his overalls and rolled his eyes upward as his body was dragged across the edge of the wagon and then fell to the hard ground with a thud. He started to protest, but soon had to deal with rocks and other sharp objects poking and scratching his back as his father pulled him into the barn and then tossed him against the wall.

"Why did you do that to me? I work hard to support you and give you a better life, and you sneak off to town and make a fool out of me. How will I ever be able to show my face after what you boys did! You are going to pay for what you did, young man!"

"But" George started, only to be immediately silenced by an open palm to the side of his face.

"Shut your damn mouth and listen to me," his father raged. "You will never do anything like that again. You are going to pay for what you did!"

At some point his father stopped speaking and just continued to emit what sounded like sobbing and rage and sadness all mixed together, as he used whatever he could find to rain down blow after blow on whatever part of George's body happened to be exposed at the time. As the rage continued, George stopped crying and just struggled to catch his breath until he eventually passed out from the pain.

The first thing he said when he awoke the next morning was, "I'm sorry." He didn't notice his mother seated next to him. Apparently, Betty Popper had been nursing her son's wounds because he noticed a blood-stained washcloth in her hand. He couldn't say anything else at that time. He just fell back asleep ashamed but unable to make amends.

George opened his eyes to the present. It was one of the memories that George replayed in his mind occasionally whenever something touched him. Maybe it was part of the reason he didn't like getting emotional. He had fond memories, and he was building many more great ones, but something inside him was stuck in the past. There were parts of him that just couldn't move forward because of what had happened to him.

Projects like digging out the basement and learning about wines and hunting helped somewhat. It kept him distracted long enough not to relive the past. The town folk had a saying, "Let sleeping dogs lie." He used it as a makeshift band-aid for his trauma, but it didn't always work. The dogs in his past woke up anyway, and he couldn't do much to stop them. He was gaining enough experience though to begin to understand what didn't work and ignoring the past didn't seem to do anything significant except buy him some time.

Because of his event-filled night and his nocturnal visit to the past, he slipped out early to do the few chores he had at the family farm. He didn't want to experience his father today, and he was hoping to somehow navigate a nap later, so he didn't want to waste any time. He finished his chores and was about to leave when he noticed his mother on the porch. He trotted up to her quickly and kissed her on the cheek before backing away to demonstrate his urgency.

"I have a thousand things to do, Mom," he said. "Love you, we'll see ya soon. Come up to the restaurant. Ricky will make you something special."

"You know your father doesn't like to come to town that much," she said shamefully.

They both just kind of gazed down and then glanced at each other apologetically. He walked away without a word, not wanting his emotions to bubble up anymore. He had experienced so much in the last 24 hours, he wished he could just go do something that would take his mind off all this. When he got like this, time passed quickly, and he found himself back at the hotel experiencing the distinct smell of breakfast.

BREAKFAST AND
GOODBYES

THE RESTAURANT WAS ALREADY FILLING WITH GUESTS ready for a hot breakfast. The men convened in the new conference room, and he thought he noticed Alesa bringing them juice and breakfast, but he was interrupted by J.D. coming down the stairs.

"Hey, your wife loaned me one of your shirts, so I could get down the road. I got a shower and I feel much better. I sincerely appreciate you listening to me last night. I won't forget it! I mean it."

The men stared into each other's eyes knowing that a bond was being built between them. It had little to do with religion or politics or economic status. It was about the human condition and how we hurt and experience things that traumatize us. They shared this experience, and it was like they were acknowledging that silently. Without warning, J.D. embraced the younger man warmly and held it for just the right amount of time.

Their heartbeats seemed to synchronize. This was the start of something new.

"You know I could save you some money on your liquor," J.D. offered.

"Oh, yeah?" George questioned.

"I gotta run," J.D. reminded him and just like that he was gone.

As George made his way back to the room, he turned and peered over his shoulder and again pondered the unusual night. The other men were chatting and discussing plans for the day. Bags were packed and placed by the entrance. Their crowd was less than half of last night, and Conrad was nowhere to be found. At least, that was what he thought until he emerged from the basement.

"Hey, George I checked out your wine cellar, if that's what you call it! It needs some work, but J.D. said we might be able to do some business, so possibly we could help get it up to snuff."

"Well, uh, okay, yeah, maybe," George fumbled around with words, but Conrad was already off on a different mission.

"Hello honey," Alesa said as she carried the last of the breakfast items to the men.

"What a night!" she continued. "That had to be the biggest night in the history of the hotel. The can is overflowing, and these guys all have ideas to make this place better. You should talk to some of them! I peeked out of the room and saw you talking to J.D. last night. You guys are going to be friends!"

After the rest left, Conrad reappeared and settled all the bills. He held out another tip for the couple, but this time Alesa stopped him.

"Hey, I tell you what! See that lady over there with two kids! She couldn't afford breakfast today, and I don't want to make a huge deal about it, but why don't you see if you can give her that money and make her feel happy about it," Alesa challenged the over-achiever.

Conrad acknowledged her challenge, accepted, and proceeded into the restaurant where the woman frantically attempted to calm her rowdy children as they ate quickly and simultaneously played with their food. George and Alesa smiled from their vantage point and saw him slyly slip the money into the woman's purse while he chatted it up with them and entertained the children.

George and Alesa had a few other things to do, so they scurried off only to return later and find that Conrad had already left. He wasn't the hugging type either, they supposed. He was warm and friendly but happier, like George, to be doing something other than talking. They noticed a handwritten note on a card on the counter. It simply said, "See you soon," and the card read, "J.D. Enterprises."

"I don't even know what they do," George offered. "I heard them mention general terms like 'distribution' and 'receipts' and all that, but I never got a chance to ask them directly what J.D. Enterprises does. I will ask next time! I think they'll be back."

Alesa slipped her arms around her husband, sneaking them into his overalls, and laid her head on his chest. They were both exhausted, but they drew a little strength and comfort from their halfhearted embrace. Alesa returned to the counter and continued totaling up receipts, putting everything back in its proper place, as George plopped on the couch just around the corner in the conference room. She thought about her parents and the fact that she and George couldn't have kids. The snores from behind her made her smile. He had fallen asleep on the couch in the middle of a sentence talking to himself. Thankfully, he didn't think about his father this time.

It was almost noon before he woke up to find Alesa curled next to him snoring like she often does when she is tired. The doors to the conference room were closed, and he reveled in the moment as he heard new guests arriving outside and Nancy greeting them warmly.

"We should get up," she said. "Don't want anyone to see us being lazy."

"You know, it sounds like everything's under control out there," he said, letting his eyes do the rest of the talking.

She looked up with wide, innocent eyes, then smiled devilishly, and led him back to the apartment. It was about two hours before someone knocked on the door. By then, they were fresh and ready to face the world.

"It's the busybody queen," Nancy said sarcastically. "She insists on talking to you guys."

This would undoubtedly be a conversation that went nowhere, but it was a part of the responsibility they had in a small town. They reaped the benefits of low crime and friendliness, but they also had to deal with the other side of that equation including the people that just didn't have enough to do. They weren't wrong, the meeting sucked, but they were able to laugh about it later. They went back to running the business and doing the things they did that made them happy, but they somehow both sensed they were moving into a new era.

Later, the young mother would ask them about the donation, but they would play it off perfectly. They had a quick meeting with all the staff to thank them for last night and challenge them to offer up ideas for the future. But mostly they just talked like a normal family right up until they all had to rush off to their usual duties.

The couple felt a twinge of gratitude and then returned to their normal routine. That is, until about a week later when the unusual shipment arrived.

DECEMBER 1925 — A NEW DAY DAWNING

"Hey there's a new delivery out back," Nancy nonchalantly blurted out.

"What? We're not expecting anything," Alesa said. "George!"

George reluctantly walked to the back door and closed it behind him. The delivery truck was unmarked but new. The driver was enthusiastic but respectful.

"Mr. Popper, J.D. sent some *giggle water* up for you to try out. He says you can have it on credit and here is the price list. We think you will be pleased and find it to be the highest quality," the driver announced.

After prohibition started, supplies of alcohol got harder and harder to procure. The prices increased as George's inventory decreased. As he scanned the price list, he was shocked. When he gazed into the back of the truck, he realized that this might be a year's supply. He couldn't get this anywhere for these prices. In a way it seemed like a gift.

"But we didn't agree on anything—he just mentioned it," George said.

"Yeah, the boss doesn't negotiate much," the driver said. "Mostly because he is offering you a deal you can't refuse. If I were you, I would take the offer, because he didn't give me permission to bring it back. Supply chains are complicated, and it would just be better for everyone if you let me unload it, and I'll be on my way."

"Okay," George reluctantly agreed, "Unload it into the wine cellar, and I'll find a way to explain it to the wife. If I flick the light, it means someone is coming. I'll send Ricky out to help you unload."

George walked slowly into the hotel lobby. Nancy was busy with a customer, so George answered the phone. He hated talking on the phone, but everyone else was somewhere else.

"Hotel Popper," George bellowed.

"George, it's J.D. How are you, my friend?"

"I'm fine, I just got the shipment of alcohol that I didn't order. What's up with that?"

"Well, listen, my friend, I knew this was a deal you couldn't refuse. A truck crashed here in the city, and I got that for rock bottom prices. I got five times that much, but I had some other obligations. Though, after your kindness to me, I would pass the savings to you. I had to move it quickly, and I meant to call you ahead of time, but there were too many irons in the fire."

Unlike their earlier visit, J.D. was much more in *go* mode today. He was talking faster and rode the wave of excitement. George couldn't help agreeing to take the alcohol because he had spent the better part of yesterday not being able to find any alcohol to sell. Poor quality and soaring prices hurt, but this checked all the boxes.

"I appreciated it, my friend! Thank you!

"Hey George," J.D. continued, "There's something else I wanted to talk to you about. Is this a good time?"

"Go ahead, man," George said and instinctively sat down.

He briefly reflected that he barely even knew this man, and they were talking business and having long phone conversations. He wondered to himself, *What is happening to me?* But another part of him already cared for this man because of the deep experience they had in the conference room. He took a deep breath and listened with all the attention he could muster. This was so unnatural for him!

"George, my nephew got in some trouble a couple of years ago. He's a fairly normal kid, but he went to prison for ... well ... some unquestionable business practices. He just got a little impatient and took some shortcuts and he finally got out the other day. We're so happy that is over for him."

"Well, give him my best," George said. "Perhaps he takes after his uncle in the whole getting ahead of himself kind of thing. I'm just kidding, sort of."

"Ha, I know and I guarantee you, George, everything I do is well-thought-out and calculated, including my reason for telling you this. I was thinking about the fact that you are remodeling the conference room. I would love for you to have a beautiful ballroom that could be used for various functions. You need someone to get the project done for you. But that's one of those things you want done by a professional."

"Yeah," George interrupted, "But I can't even afford to do it myself. Well, I could, but we don't want to spend that kind of money for my quality of work. It's kind of like the booze situation—too much money for the lowest quality."

"Exactly," J.D. chimed back in, "that is exactly the reason my solution makes so much sense."

"What solution? What are you talking about?"

"I'm getting there. Be patient, don't interrupt me, and I'll lay it all out for you. Okay, my nephew is one of the premier contractors in the city, but his reputation is a little tarnished. He doesn't have many living expenses now, so here is what I'm proposing. If you can find a space for him to sleep, he would be willing to work for you for free so that he can make a fresh start, get some experience in another area, and get his legs under him. I think a small town would be healing for him and you guys would be a positive influence on him like you are the rest of your employees."

George was about to tap out on conversation for today. Alesa, now in the room, kept looking at him and trying to ask him who he was talking to. He wasn't particularly practiced at this, and it was stressing him out. He would have handed her the phone, but J.D. was already deep into the story, and he didn't want him to have to start over.

"George, listen! At the end of this project, you would have a ballroom and conference room that would be the envy of every hotel within a hundred miles and all it would cost you was materials. Or, you could have one that you design that is more like the wine cellar. And, speaking of the wine cellar … maybe … "

George sensed a lull in the storm of the conversation and offered, "Okay, let me get this straight. Your nephew will basically become my adopted brother for a while. In his spare time, we get a world-class ballroom. Are you sure there's not some danger in this, like introducing a criminal to our community?"

"Lyle is not a criminal," J.D. said defensively.

"Well, he did commit a crime and served his time."

"Fair enough," J.D. said, "but, what he did was barely illegal, and he is my nephew. He just needs a fresh start. I know you're going out on a limb, but I'm doing the same by sending you all that booze. Trust me this time and you'll see. It's going to benefit both of us and vault you into the next level at the hotel. My nephew will take your hotel, not just the ballroom, to a new level."

"Okay, when are you going to send him?"

"He's already on the bus, headed your way," J.D. said apologetically. "I had a backup plan, but I was hoping you would say yes."

George just hung his head and chuckled—it was all you could do with J.D. he conceded. He said goodbye and readied himself for what was ahead. He had just made two major decisions without consulting his partner and wife. His only ace in the hole was that she liked J.D., a lot. He was almost like a good father, at least that's what she thought when she met him recently. He was hoping she was as mesmerized by their new friends as he was. Despite this, he was still going to be in trouble. They didn't fight much, but when they did, it was usually an event.

He whispered to himself, "Ding, ding, ding ... here we go!"

She had waited patiently for the call to end, but that was waning.

"Sit down, Alesa, we have to talk," George said with as much compassion as he could muster.

"Am I in trouble," she smiled, which was funny because she never got in trouble; it was always George.

"No, you are not in trouble, but I made a couple of decisions without you," he began, "but it's not my fault."

"Well, whose fault is it?"

"Scratch that. It is my fault, totally my fault. But I don't think it's bad. And J.D. is the one that talked me into it."

"Where is he ... Is he here?" she said, looking around worriedly.

"Should I be worried?" George questioned.

"Remember you are the one in trouble here," she said. "I know what you mean. What did he talk you into? Are we going to have to sell the hotel? Did you sleep with a prostitute? Do I need a lawyer?"

"Calm down, it's nothing like that."

"Don't tell me to calm down, you know I hate when you dismiss my feelings."

George took a second to regroup. The one thing that he didn't want to do is create more problems just because of this. He was in enough trouble for not involving her in the decisions. Women had just obtained the right to vote, and no one was happier about that than Alesa. But she just didn't want to vote for a president; she wanted an equal say in how they ran the business. They were partners and she would not be diminished!

"Let's take this one thing at a time," he began.

"How many things are there?" she interrupted again.

"Please let me finish," he said with authority. "J.D. mentioned getting us better deals on the liquor when he was here. He took it upon himself to send a shipment that should last us until the end of the year. It's an unbelievably fantastic deal. I don't even know how he got it, and I don't care. It has been so hard to get liquor since prohibition began, and I think it's going to be a godsend that he did. I was wondering what we were going to do, and it showed up at the right time. If I was religious, I might thank God, but in this case, I think we should thank J.D. Enterprises. The only thing he did wrong was not tell us ahead of time. I can punish him for that, but then we are most likely out of business on the alcohol home front."

"I totally agree with your decision," she said carefully, "but, additionally I trust J.D. a little less, and I will have a word with him when I see him next. I'm going to give both of you a free pass on this one based on what you tell me next. If the next one is a stupid idea, I may remove my vote and kick J.D.'s ass next time I see him. Are we clear?"

George smiled a little. He knew it was a little patronizing to like it when she got assertive, but he couldn't help it. He knew it was a part of her childhood and the dysfunction that many feel, but it was one of the things he liked about her. He just didn't want to feel too much of her aggression, of course unless it benefited him sexually. According to her, everything for him was rooted in sex. So, even though he was deadly serious about the second issue, he was also smiling at her which only made her a little angrier.

"Okay, the second thing that happened when J.D. called was…"

"J.D. *called?* why didn't you tell me."

"Again, should I be worried?"

"Continue," she said, waving her hand.

"Okay, J.D.'s nephew is being released from prison. He did something minor and used to be one of the best contractors in the city. He took a few shortcuts and got put in jail and was just released last week. He is willing to do carpentry work for us for free for however long it takes to get our projects done and to rehabilitate him and give him a fresh start. So, if we give him a place to stay, room and board, and let him work for us, we can essentially have a contractor for free and transform this hotel into a next level hotel."

"But he didn't ask us, he just told us to do it. So, how long do we have to agree?"

"I already agreed, and he's probably on the bus."

And that did it. She stormed off into the bedroom. George had the sinking feeling he had won a battle and lost the war. He investigated the backroom and saw her throwing things and walking back and forth muttering to herself. He knew this wasn't going to be easy, but she surprised him and charged back into the room aiming her finger at his chest like a bayonet.

"Okay listen to me," she began. "Both of these ideas are fantastic except for a few things like this nephew may attack me in my sleep, and J.D. may just be setting us up for later or something. But on the surface, we need to make some changes, and these two things may give us that boost we need to keep doing this into the future with some success. Please don't start smiling again, or I may smash your face in. Let me just say if you and J.D. cook up another one of these plans and don't include me, I'm going to go crazy. I will not be ignored!"

"Understood," the man of few words said, softly.

About that time, Ricky brought them both a well-needed drink. They toasted each other as was their custom, and the rest of the staff breathed a collective sigh of relief. George checked around the lobby and the restaurant to make sure everyone was still okay after the battle. He quietly swept up some broken glass and put down a towel to soak up the water from the fractured vase. Nobody noticed Alesa had slipped away until they heard her talking on the phone.

"Hi J.D, this Alesa at the hotel—yes, yes—listen, the next time you and George make a decision that involves me, could you make sure I am in the meeting? Thank you, I appreciate your understanding."

The whole staff smiled as Alesa headed off for a hot bath. They knew she was done—she had her final say. They all hoped the new decision was a wise one.

For the next few years, they prospered exceptionally. Lyle finished the ballroom quickly, and it was stunning. They impressed every guest with a quick tour. After that, he fixed everything that was broken, gave the hotel a classy update, and even tied it all together with a coherent theme. The success helped him establish his own business in town, and with a few slight adjustments to small town customs, he began to fit in and thrive.

The couple, their hotel, and the town thrived for a few more years. Hotel Popper was known as the best hostel in a hundred miles. The unconventional locale was the place to be, where the biggest names stopped on their way to whatever lay beyond town limits, and where others gathered for a getaway.

Business was prosperous until it wasn't—namely, the times got especially challenging in 1929 when that little mess in New York suddenly became the Great Depression, and no one was spared.

BACK TO THE FUTURE

SOME QUICK MATH EARLY ON HAD INFORMED JOE THE hotel existed a little over a century. So, it was impossible to find someone that was an adult and cognizant of that time when the Poppers owners might have been apt to dig tunnels. Joe guessed that this was during Prohibition which took place during the 1920s and 1930s.

Briefly, Joe thought of Carrie A. Nation. Originally born Carrie Amelia Moore from Kansas. Nation's first husband drank himself to death after his very pregnant wife left him because of his alcoholism. She would later become a well-known activist against alcohol and was even referred to as "Mother Nation" by her temperate sisters. She eventually traveled the country smashing up bars with a hatchet, giving speeches against the dangers of alcohol, and bailing herself out of jail from the fees she charged for selling souvenir hatchets. She was an important figure not only in the temperance movement, but her work later influenced support for Prohibition and women's right to vote. For just a moment, Joe envisioned Carrie coming to his hometown during the early 1900s and smashing up the liquor establishments.

He thought about this when he considered his current plight. Why did he want to find out about the hotel, and what was true about that hotel? To some degree, we all have causes we care about. These causes are motivated in part by situations in our lives. For Carrie, her husband's demise motivated her to do something about what she saw as social injustice. It was extreme, but it brought attention to the subject, and when she found others that agreed with her, a movement was born.

Joe also thought about the fact that most organizations develop systemic problems. He assumed this was true for towns, cities, nations, and people groups. As the systemic problems develop, they become ingrained in the practices of the people in those organizations and become somewhat normal. The organizations realize they have some issues, but traditions and practices are normalized and changing often is like anarchy and isn't considered for long. Joe knew this from his years as a deacon. No one wanted to risk the good things they had to root out the problematic issues.

As Joe examined his entire life, he realized he had experienced some unfairness. He was raised fairly poor, had vision issues, and came from areas of the country that didn't fully understand racism and other social issues. He always felt like he was behind and trying to play catch up. He longed for a father figure that would give him a shortcut or some magic solution to make life fairer and easier to navigate. He never fully discovered the silver bullet, but assumed most people struggle in this area because religion, at its core, is trying to address these issues.

He longed to have the "right" information philosophically and spiritually. For years, he struggled with Scripture and Theology because he wanted people to know the right way to approach and find God. After struggling to find the right formula, he was beginning to realize that Scripture wasn't necessarily written precisely, and hard as he tried, it wouldn't fit neatly into a box or magic solution. There were tens of thousands of Protestant denominations that all believed they were right, but just asking a few poignant questions could quickly raise doubts about infallibility.

He also seemed to be on a quest for the right intellectual information. Joe loved to learn. Every time he discovered something, he felt like he had gained access into a new realm of humanity. But just as he might have an epiphany, he realized those in his *circles* may not grasp that information yet, so he either had to educate them or wait for them to internalize it at a snail's pace. It was frustrating, and he struggled to not be arrogant or condescending toward those that simply hadn't had the opportunity to learn what he had recently become aware of.

Joe's latest endeavor brought him closer to understanding more about the effects of trauma. He didn't fully conceptualize it yet, but after years in a small town and decades of time on earth, he found most people had experienced some type of trauma in their lives that continued to affect them throughout. It didn't just dissipate when they ignored it either, and consistent denial made it worse. From organized religion, he realized that when trauma is unaddressed, it is propagated towards others. Hurt people hurt other people and create problems for all. Small towns are very aware of each other, but often dismissive of the systemic issues they face.

So, the motivations that might be leading to Joe's desire to learn about the hotel were complicated. If he had to boil it down to one thing, he thought, it is probably just that he liked *adventure*. He loved that each discovery could hopefully help someone else. The thrill of skydiving fueled him to start a club that introduced more thrill seekers to this unbelievable adrenaline rush. The nature of religion led him to evangelism in order to recruit lost souls to the fold. Therefore, revealing the rightful history of this sleepy town might help encourage its residents to embrace a more authentic identity. Even if it wasn't what they imagined, it should be true and honest.

And that was it! He had a deep desire for all to be *authentic*.

He held this thought, even penning it, because he wanted to share it verbatim with George. There were still a few days before their next visit. He didn't necessarily feel a deep desire to be overly concise, but it was helpful to have something he could at least articulate to others.

After assessing the list of residents that might have more information, his introverted nature kicked in and the dread began. This part of the process involved small talk. Joe would rather introduce two people, let them start their conversation, and then slip away. But, at the moment, he was the only one motivated to probe further, and he would have to be a reporter whether he wanted to or not. He put it off for a couple of hours, then he finally made the first call.

THE OLDIES

EVEN THOUGH JOE ADORED HIS MOTHER, HE OFTEN dreaded calling her because she was hard of hearing. She blamed it on being in the band in high school, but the why didn't matter. What did matter was that they always start conversations the same way because she either bought the cheap hearing aids or turned them down or didn't put them in to answer the phone. The conversation always began as usual:

"Hello, Mom?"

"Joey? I can hardly hear you. Wait a minute, let me get to where I get better reception."

"You should ... never mind ... okay, Mom!"

"Can you hear me now?"

"Me hearing is not usually the problem. Can you hear me?"

"What, wait a minute, let me put my hearing aids in ... Just a minute I can't hear a thing."

Joe would pace the house, rub his face in bubbling frustration, and wait well over a minute for his 70-year-old mother to get it together. Other than talking on the phone, she was highly functioning, did good deeds for the less fortunate, and was well-respected around town. They did argue about political views, but only on Facebook because face-to-face confrontation was never the family thing. His anger and frustration would then reach an unnecessary peak, and he would flail the wrong arm causing his phone to tumble down the stairs onto his porch and somehow hang up (yes, every time). He'd mumble a few curses, blame her in the recesses of his mind, and then call her back, pleading to God that there would be no repeat of the first five minutes.

"Hello, Mom! Can you hear me now?"

"Who is this?"

"It's me, Joey! I just called you!" he would chuckle, nearing insanity at that point. *"Oh, since you hung up on me, I thought you were mad at me."*

"I am mad at … mom … Do you have your hearing aid now?" Joe would practically shout.

"Yes, let me turn them up."

Thinking back at this moment, Joe couldn't help but wonder if this was payback for something he did as a kid. He could picture his kind, sweet mother plotting to get back at him—it was part of the shame he lived with though considered normal. But more likely she was just a 70-year-old woman, not Superwoman, and some things were starting to slip a little whether either of them wanted to admit it.

Suddenly, Joe realized his contact list contained several older individuals who may share his mother's limitations, thus forcing him into one of Dante's circles of hell to endlessly repeat this conversation (there must be one like this). He already regretted making this first call. Even though Aaron told him they were highly functioning, he had a reference point for what that meant. They were highly functioning 90 and 100-year-olds. He decided to call the older lady first. Her name was Joann.

"Mrs. Christian, this is Joe Forester," Joe began, only to be interrupted.

"Who, wait, what does that mean to me?" she spoke.

She wasn't trying to be rude. Joe could relate to answering telemarketer calls and getting phone calls he wasn't ready for. So, he interjected quickly and used Aaron's name to gain credibility which changed her demeanor. After clearing her throat a few times and turning up *her* hearing aid, Joe felt like he was speaking to one of his mother's friends which simultaneously caused him slight discomfort and a bit of dread.

She coughed a little and Joe proposed his first question.

"What do you know about the Hotel Popper?"

"Oh yeah, it's right downtown there," she began, "George was a wonderful man to the community."

"Yeah, I live just a few blocks from there," Joe added, "on Popper Street."

"Wait, where do you live? Is it near the Methodist church?"

"Yes ma'am, right across the street!"

"Is it the white house? Well, not the *White House*, but a white house. My uncle built that house. He was very meticulous. He watched every nail being put in."

"We love the house, Mrs. Christian!" he yelled, reminding himself about her hearing aids. "What do you think about all the rumors of tunnels under the street and all that?"

"Oh, I don't know, George was a decent man and generous to the town" she answered. "We used to come see a show downtown and then go to his restaurant and have a bite to eat. George helped a lot of people."

"Do you think the hotel is haunted?" Joe offered.

"Surely not," she said. "We didn't go to the hotel. We just went to the restaurant on Saturdays."

Joe just decided to have a conversation and pretend like he was talking to his mom. She was exercising her privilege as a 100-year-old woman to talk about whatever she wanted to talk about. When Joe considered that this woman had lived through both World Wars, the Great Depression, and all the tumultuous decades in the last century, he was almost embarrassed for quizzing her about the old hotel, but he figured it would give her something to talk about for a while. When she started talking about being a Sunday School teacher, Joe panicked and just tried to avoid the religion talk altogether.

"Mrs. Christian, I sure appreciate your time!"

"Oh, it was very nice to talk to you."

Thinking about conversations over the phone, and then actually talking to an older person left him exhausted, but he dialed immediately before he curled up in a fetal position. The second call was a little easier; after all she was only 90. Her answers were briefer, even though she was very friendly.

"We just didn't come to town," she kept saying.

Joe kept thinking that was ridiculous, and he wanted to ask her some tough questions, but he had been beaten down by the previous phone call and other suppressed memories trying to resurface. He connected this kind woman with people in church that told him they never struggled with *things like that.* He knew it was unfair to judge her, but he guessed that she *did* sneak into town a few times, and that secret was going to go to the grave with her. Since he stopped being a deacon, he had given up on saving everyone—which involved condemning them first. He was now content to let people live their lives for the most part.

He gave up and got off the phone and quickly called the newspaper.

"Can you tell the owner I'm just looking for pictures of the inside of the old hotel?"

After explaining what his purposes were, something in her voice told Joe the newspaper guy wasn't going to call him back any time soon. So, Joe crossed him off the list and was thankful that even though he hit a lot of dead ends, he knew some things that were not going to work. He used this approach a lot in his life. He stubbornly would dive in despite being ill-equipped to tackle whatever obstacle, but stubbornly, he would keep trying until he broke through the figurative wall. He also knew if you kick down too many of those walls in a small town, someone eventually kicks your ass in one way or another.

He didn't fault anyone that day for doing what they did or saying what they said. It helped to think of his mom first who was apt to do or say anything as well. He considered the fact that other people have issues buried deep within just like he did. Secrets aren't confined to old hotels and mysterious tunnels. Secrets are kept by individuals because they don't want to feel *that way* ever again. People have their own vantage points and perspectives, and what is important to *us* is not always important to them. Joe thought about all these things and somehow came to an acceptance that day.

All this contemplating over his mother and elderly women made him also think about his father and the regrets he had there. Joe had been piecing together bits of information about George Popper's father, and it caused his imagination to run wild. The regrets he had about his relationship with his father certainly weren't foreign to most people. Relationships are hard and especially when there's extraordinarily little training on how to maintain them in the midst of the greatest hardships in American history nestled between two world wars.

There was no evidence of Bud Popper being involved in any of his son's business endeavors. Joe pondered that fact and imagined the possibilities as he fell asleep on the couch staring up at that annoying crack in the wall. He didn't get to rest long because his Australian Shepherd woke him abruptly from his sleep. Gaston was indignant that the person delivering the mail dared to invade his perimeter. When the barking subsided and Joe's heart rate finally returned to normal, he habitually picked up his phone and started scrolling.

RANDOM SEARCHES

"WAIT, WHAT?" HE SAID TO HIMSELF AS HE LEANED OVER to focus on the internet post.

Over the past few weeks, Joe had made it his habit to search, imagine, and probe into different parts of the story. He wanted to go back to the library but didn't have the time. As is the practice of modern times, he used his phone instead. The internet is not just a haven for all things negative; it also puts the information of the world at our fingertips. Research is so much easier, though possibly a little more dangerous.

Joe randomly typed on his phone, searching for whatever was coming to his mind: *Hotel Popper, George Popper, prohibition popper, etc.* Then there it was. Something that he hadn't seen in the library or any time before. None of the people he interviewed mentioned this incident and even Marla didn't know about it. He messaged her and sent her a link to the information. The fact that no one knew this story doesn't necessarily prove anything, but what Joe supposed was that it was a piece of the puzzle. The record from the state supreme court began, *O'Malley vs Popper.*

He took a deep breath realizing at the very least this could be a direct window into the past. It was dated 1934 and described an appeal case to the state supreme court over a more local case between O'Malley, a lumber yard owner, and George Popper. O'Malley accused George of assaulting him over disagreements, and when the case was decided against the plaintiff, he appealed to the higher court. The lumberyard owner was unable to prove anything other than self-defense mostly because of the corroborated evidence that O'Malley continually harassed the defendant and failed to produce witnesses for his side of the argument.

It was hard to decipher from a short case summary what happened, but Joe pieced the story together from the evidence he read.

Apparently, the issue began over the dispute of a lumber bill. Joe knew from other accounts that this might have been a time when George was making renovations to the hotel, so this made sense. Since Joe knew about small-town life, he was familiar with how these things play out. Most often, people can't afford expensive legal remedies, so they rely on the court of public opinion. If the general perception of the person you are *against* is decent, then you must lower that perception in the mind of the town people by spreading rumors or publicly shaming them.

Most likely, because George didn't agree with the bill, he refused to pay it to make a point. It wasn't likely that he totally refused to pay it because there were probably only one or two lumber yards in town, and the word gets around fast. If you don't pay your bills, it's hard to do business.

So, at some point in the feud, Mr. O'Malley grew disappointed with George and considered him as a menace not just a person that owed money. Because O'Malley disagreed with the business owner, George became an enemy that needed to be removed. Most of us can relate to these escalations. They happen every day on social media. It dawned on Joe that is what happened in his relationship with Charlie, so he took a moment to send him a *friend request.*

On the day of the incident, several of George's friends were sitting on the front porch of the hotel when O'Malley went into the bank on the other side of the street. As he came out, one man called, "There he is!"

To this, O'Malley replied, "You, bootlegging, son-of-a-bitch! I thought you were honest. You can't be honest and work over there!"

From the record, several residents testified that O'Malley had been repeating these slanders for several weeks. He could be heard to say, "I'm going to do everything I can to stop that Dutchman bastard," implying George was the source of all evil in the town through his hotel, restaurant, and other businesses.

On the day in question, he stopped in front of the bank to write on a piece of paper which later was identified as writing down the license plates from cars in front of the hotel. He had previously reported to neighboring states and the state supervisor of liquor control that illegal liquor sales were regularly happening right there at the hotel. Subsequent investigations failed to turn up any tangible evidence of criminal behavior.

George did indeed cross the street that day after restraining one of his friends that wanted to "take care of this guy!" But, after that fact, there is a dispute of what happened next. O'Malley claims that George "punched him in the face and slammed him down on the concrete causing a concussion." George claims that he was only defending himself from the overexcited crusader of public protection that was out to destroy him.

Joe surmised that there were probably a lot of things that were interesting about that day. Two men had forgotten civility and instead chose to treat each other as enemies. Both probably considered themselves morally superior. Joe knew from his time as a deacon that it was easy to demonize the "other" and consider all kinds of unreasonable acts to "get rid" of what is causing consternation. He had witnessed the ugliest of behavior between two deacons that were supposed to be the leaders of the faith community.

Moreover, he knew from human nature that both men were probably at fault. George could have handled the situation better by privately discussing the bill rather than publicly embarrassing the lumberyard owner. As things escalated, an arbitrator might have been helpful to discuss the situation rationally. To Joe, many of these situations boiled down to the way we categorize the people that are against us and forget that we are all a part of the same team.

Joe imagined that George probably just wanted to go back to the river and *wrestle* this thing out. In his own life, he often imagined this to be true. But then he remembered puberty and the awkwardness of youth and realized, none of it is simple; it's simply different. From the time we reach out for the other child's toy and scream "Mine!", we navigate the minefield of difficult human relations. We make decisions, follow certain paths, and struggle. It's a common experience.

Joe sat in his recliner for close to two hours before Mary repeated her calls through the house, "Hello, hello, hello!"

"What are you doing over there?"

"Just thinking about life," he said softly, "Just thinking about life."

Gaston uncurled from just beneath his feet and stretched. It was clear that he wasn't thinking about anything, but he walked slowly toward Mary and acknowledged her. He considered what the next action the couple might take for just a few seconds so he could follow them. Realizing they weren't going anywhere fast; he lay down in the middle of the room and went back to sleep.

PONDERING LIFE

As Joe sorted through what he considered the *bigger things* in life, he couldn't help but notice that he had mostly questions and very few answers. Though he had learned how to question or challenge what he didn't understand, part of him was ashamed that he was over 50 and still hadn't gotten it all figured out. It was common for him to feel behind and in need of progression toward his goals. He always felt disadvantaged, and he used that for motivation to work harder or smarter or whatever the popular mantra was. For him, it was just the fuel that drove him. "I'll show them!" was his battle cry.

But recently, especially after he stepped away from organized religion, he really thought things through. Some had to do with religion, some about the bigger questions of life and what matters most. Because he read about the court case, he also thought about the reality that under certain conditions, a single disagreement between a fellow human being can become what matters more than life itself. In the heat of the battle, George and O'Malley couldn't imagine that anything mattered more than being right. What makes us like that? What makes us do those things?

O'Malley vs Popper prompted Joe to examine it all.

He examined his *certainty* through a religious lens. For the last few years, Joe had been on this journey of discovery. His tradition taught him to be certain about everything theological. The systematic theology they had embraced was considered close to flawless and made so much sense that they could claim with certainty their *non-negotiables*. But he also came to realize that there were tens of thousands of religious organizations that all believed they were right, and their essentials were righter than everyone else's.

A Benedictine nun once told Joe, "No one is right." This shook him to the core because he had previously entertained a simple thought, *What if I am wrong?* He remained uneasy that there were uncertainties regarding his belief. However, he considered it worse to affirm that which he wasn't convinced was true. It was better now to think simplistically of religion as an attempt to understand the Divine. He supposed that was what those writers of the sacred texts attempted, but more often than not they drew arbitrary lines in the sand for whatever reason, which usually arrested creativity and understanding and the quest for truth.

Not knowing all the answers (for once) kept Joe searching. He was beginning to realize that part of the adventure is not knowing where you were headed. He had so many questions about religion that he considered starting a journal of them all.

Joe was middle aged, and he noticed some major themes emerging. Some words or ideas began to matter more. There were subjects and concepts and *truths* that threaded consistently through time and even in key moments of his life. They didn't always catch his attention until he saw them in various poignant circumstances of his story.

For example, *compassion.* Joe remembered that when Jesus traveled through Galilee, he often saw a congregation of people and felt compassion for them. That was kind of insignificant until Joe asked a friend what he should do about someone that was disagreeing with him. The friend suggested having compassion for them. And then later when he did some internal work, someone else suggested further that he might need to have compassion for himself. It was significant not because it was a stated or standard doctrine or rule, but because it was common and effective for the journey.

George and O'Malley might have been spared from this perma-
nent record of their altercation and public disgrace with just a small
amount of compassion for each other.

And what of *retribution?* Reacting versus responding was the worst
possible human response to him. Throughout the years, when Mary
would trigger him inadvertently, the worst thing he could do was react
and respond with retribution. But most religious systems seem to be
based on that basic idea that God or whatever they call "god," is simply responding to our actions and paying us back—retribution!

Hell was always the starting place for Joe's religion because they
assumed we were all bad originally and required God to punish us for
that. But Joe was having a much harder time accepting that because
he couldn't imagine God was worse than him anymore. If it were the
worst thing for him to respond to the actions of his family with retribution (revenge, etc.), how could it be holy for the Divine to act that
way? How could God be restorative and retributive at the same time?

His parents and religious teachers taught him not to be retributive
based on the sacred writings, but then they also showed him that God
was apparently that way and even worse. It made sense in his childhood that God was somewhat like him, but as he and his mindset
matured, he imagined that God should be *better* than him. He often
said aloud, "God cannot have a worse temper than me, and he can't
be more retributive than I am."

He no longer allowed people to excuse these types of questions
away because they were hard to answer. Joe was beginning to be comfortable searching for better answers than he was being satisfied with
what was once easy to accept.

Because Joe came from a Christian background, he was quite
familiar with the basic ideas that Jesus taught. The simple injunction
to love God and love our neighbor and treat people like you want
to be treated made perfect sense and could be a totally appropriate
way to live his life. Unfortunately, many of the congregation he knew

sacrificed these ideals on the altars of politics, the business of religion, and their own struggle for significance. He included himself as an offender, but he couldn't be comfortable with it any longer.

He felt many people had come to this nexus in their lives, but he longed for the systems and organizations around him to collectively adopt a better way. He imagined this was what Jesus and other leaders also imagined but never saw it realized.

When Joe considered the business of religion, he couldn't help but be disillusioned. He longed to be communal in a way that made more sense. The multi-million-dollar enterprises were about the furthest thing from being effective. Even worse, in his opinion, the trauma they produced not only damaged but reproduced subsequent inherited trauma in others. And the answer could not be to return to those original models as they wouldn't be effective in this modern, globalized time.

But every time he tried to talk about this, someone like Charlie would come out of the woodwork and accuse him of hating the church. Those invested in organized religion would talk about progress or adaptation, probably, he assumed, because they were used to easy answers and were penalized for asking questions. In his mind, it was going to take a re-imagining or a reengineering of the entire process. Like his faith journey, there might need to be some deconstruction or demolition of the current system, and he knew that most people inside of those faith organizations could not afford to even have that conversation.

He once supposed that a lot of these issues are based in *fear* for whatever reason. Most religions originate this way as a means to convince their followers to adopt their solution. Joe didn't believe they did this on purpose because he didn't ever intentionally provoke fear in people. But now that he looked at it from another vantage point, he realized fear is a big part of how people motivate each other. He assumed it was probably in our root brains to protect from danger, real or perceived, but he wasn't sure and didn't have the energy to tackle that significant of a question today.

Joe had always been a doer. He was a deacon in the church mostly because he just seized every possibility for action and did it with an urgency that overcame any barrier or opposition. Since he considered himself at a disadvantage, he could always use it for motivation to prove it to them. He ignored the fact that this required him to turn almost everyone into opposition. Generally, he considered these little wars a necessary part of doing business and getting things done.

Until eventually, a whisper passed through his ear that altered his trajectory.

"Joe you are a human being, not a human doing."

It was one of those things that stopped him in his tracks. Even now, he could say he daily thought over that statement. Once he would have considered *being* to be a new age term, but he now considers it a life goal that he has no idea how to pursue. Since he didn't have it figured out yet, he assumed that he wouldn't discuss it with George at the library even though he had no idea what he was going to discuss.

A recent excursion to Asia, caused him to begin a journey to understand two previously misunderstood terms: *authenticity* and *presence*.

Getting outside the comfort zone of his hometown and religion caused him to examine how trying to conform to accepted norms had damaged his ability to be who he really was. Previously, he would have without question and, without giving much thought, molded all his actions around the accepted behavior and belief of his co-workers, church members, and family. The trouble with this model, though it avoided conflict, was that it caused him to not always *act* in a way consistent with his true self.

He realized his authenticity was just now being nurtured, and so was now able to accept the mission. Somewhat dysfunctional, it aligned with his belief that he was always behind, so he proposed to work harder at being more enlightened about it, which worked for now.

Additionally, Joe struggled with finding comfortability with his own presence. As he understood it, it was best to just be than always do. It still didn't come naturally, and he absolutely had to work at it, but his friend told him to *be* and *become* and somehow that stuck. The first time he sat for 20 minutes and didn't do anything except occasionally repeat the word "stillness." It felt like an eternity. Now, he could do this more easily. He loved being productive, but the pull to achievement had somehow started to shift within him.

He tried to be present when he anticipated the next meeting with George. Lately, the people that intersected his path were more like George. They weren't people that told him what to think or how to believe, and they didn't impose their own agenda on him. The new sages in his life were people that shared their journey or helped him reveal his true self. Although he still longed for someone to tell him what to think, he was growing out of it to a more mature way of being.

He fell asleep mentally exhausted and thinking about both Georges. Gaston remained at peace on the floor.

GEORGE AND JOE
REVISITED

SINCE HE HAD A COUPLE OF HOURS TO SPARE, JOE RAN TO his now second home to research a couple of details. He wanted to see if there was a book on O'Malley like there was on the Poppers. His pessimistic side told him he wasn't going to find anything significant. He also wanted to try to reconnect with George and didn't know how, so mostly he was grasping at straws.

He was right; no book or notes on O'Malley. He probably left after the incident. Feuds generally aren't resolved, and since most of his current research friends had never heard the name, O'Malley probably sold out and went somewhere else. The records showed that 30 years later, George Popper was still thriving in the town. Perhaps the two worked out their differences, and each lived happily ever after. But realistically, if Popper survived, O'Malley probably didn't. Joe weighed the possibility of something much more dramatic and seedier, but he let it go.

Instead, he made his way to the front desk. This time he noticed the name plate and addressed the quaint woman directly.

"Hey Sara, how are you?"

"Are you *still* trying to find information about the Popper Hotel?" she interrupted.

"Yeah, I talked to a few of the locals that are older, but unfortunately, I probably needed to talk to their parents about 20 years ago. It doesn't seem like anyone cares too much about remembering that time frame. That just makes it more interesting to me, but I wish it were easier."

"I agree with you," Sara said. "It's interesting but I don't care. I mean even if the guy killed someone, I don't care about the past. I try not to judge anyone, and I get my adventure from the novels."

"Yeah, the most interesting mystery for me," Joe stated inquisitively, "is why do I care so much? People keep saying the town has secrets, but why do I care about that? In fact, that is what the dude I met in here the other day said I should figure out."

"Oh, speaking of him. He was in here earlier."

"Shoot, you mean I just missed him?" Joe said, hanging his head and at the same time wondering why he cared about any of this. Most times he was content just to be at home and write, but for some reason, he wanted to unravel the mystery and deliver answers to the old man.

"He said he was going to supper and would be back before we closed," Sara assured him.

"That's great, I'll wait in the genealogy room. Will you tell him I'm here?"

"Yes sir, Mr. Detective," she mocked.

She wasn't sarcastic, just more intrigued by his continual pursuits, and she wasn't lying. She didn't care and was already back to her novel before he turned away. Other patrons searched the shelves for their next read. It always surprised Joe that people still actually came to the library, but he was glad there were readers since he was a writer. The misnomer was that with the digital age there was less reading, but Joe supposed the opposite when the world was literally at their fingertips.

Joe was partly anxious because he didn't have an appealing answer for George. He didn't know what the man wanted from him. He could have said "answers," but then he would have to know what the question was. His interests were piqued, and he was engaged in the adventure, but he couldn't identify why it was important to him.

Over the past few weeks, he noticed some unique things that had been coming to the surface. The first, right after meeting with George, was the idea of *being*. Since his trip to Asia, he had been investigating this consistently. It was common for Joe to get most of his validation from the things he did, but just to "be," was a whole other matter. He knew this adventure at the hotel posed several challenges to this thought process.

When Joe considered his next step in this journey, he was often confronted with the dilemma of *should I go do something (interview, research, look) or should I just sit with the information I already have*. He was finding that life is a journey of being and becoming as much as it is of doing. Obviously, we don't ever quit actively doing, but learning to be where we are was becoming increasingly important to Joe, and he was beginning to understand its value.

Part of being for Joe was writing. When he would write, his mind opened up to all possibilities and allowed him to think deeply about the past and how it relates to the future. He was even considering how in some ways the hotel might be a metaphor or somehow correlate to issues in our lives. Every blog he wrote also ended with something he learned by being and becoming.

He was also discovering that he could still be proactive and diligent, but time spent being mindful and just being, was not time wasted. It was valuable and productive in its own way. His new practice of contemplative prayer and mindfulness kept his energy flowing toward the right things and opened himself up to healing and growth and all kinds of new internal quests. His religion had tried to bring him certainty and simplicity, where his newfound practices introduced mystery, nuance, and paradox to his ever-evolving way of being. He was finding real joy and lasting peace simply from being where he was.

The significance of understanding what was *urgent* and what was *important* enthralled him. This comparison had surfaced many times in his life at critical junctures. Like when he was first married and realized the things that he thought were urgent, like his hobbies, had to now be subservient to what was important because he was now married. Also, when his children were born, the priorities shifted again. New jobs, new churches, and new hobbies all moved the needle on what was urgent and what was important.

But, as he entered the second half of life and relied less and less on ego to guide him, he realized there was then less and less that he was *required* to do. He was able to see more of the bigger picture—he had no one to impress; no one he needed to prove things to; and most things could wait until tomorrow. Even when he was proactive and responsible, there were fewer demands of his immediate attention. So, that makes it easier right?

Well, what Joe realized was that with less pressure from the external stimuli, he was now forced to make even better choices with what he allowed to be urgent. Since he had time to focus intently on this mystery or adventure at the hotel, which parts of it are urgent and what parts are important? Maybe, it ties back to being. When did he need to just be and when did he need to do something?

His last contract job paid him a lot of money. Since cutting expenses and living a simpler life, he was able to save much of it. He contemplated that maybe one day he should return to a normal job since his blog was not yet "viral." But did he need to get back to a normal job or were there other forces speaking urgency when he needed to think about what is important. Might there be a life lesson somewhere in this experience that was worth more?

Instead, he turned his attention to the idea of *what matters most.* To begin with, Joe considered what mattered most to the people in town he was interviewing. Most people in a small town enjoy the fact that nothing ever happens. There are a predictable number of activities, the same ones repeated annually that bring a certain amount of stability. It may be a false sense of security, but it works to some extent, so it matters a lot to life-long residents.

Joe noticed this in the people he interviewed. They all remembered something different, but what they recalled was what mattered the most to them. This not only affected what they remember but how they live their lives. They were willing to speak up about or get angry about or lose sleep over what they treasured. Being a deacon for two decades, Joe saw numerous examples of people fighting vehemently for something that appeared insignificant, but he now realized it was what mattered most to them. He realized we all choose, through the lens of our history, what we will place on the altar of importance. It is, in a sense, what is God to us.

What mattered most to O'Malley was completely opposite of what mattered most to Popper. The men weren't all that different. They both were about the same age, ran businesses, were grandchildren of immigrants, and had nearly the same basic religious beliefs. But certain things that *mattered most* became so large in their eyes that they categorized their neighbor as *other,* thereby, justifying going to war. This happens all over the world and has happened since the beginning of time.

Joe wanted to believe that the world could change. When he considered the growth he experienced over the last few years, he likened it to an *evolution.* He hadn't just changed, he felt like he was growing, moving upward, or progressing into something brand new. It felt like rebirth, and if only the whole world could experience this transition together. He believed they could because he met people every day experiencing the same evolution and becoming as he, himself felt.

He was pondering that very thought when George appeared. Joe hadn't heard him come in nor knew how long the wise man had been sitting before him. Joe was too deep in thought, and these were complicated things he couldn't quite wrangle into a theology. He both longed to figure it all out and enjoyed the sheer mystery.

"Hello, friend," George said calmly, despite the patrons shuffling books as they readied to leave before the thirty-minute closing time.

"Oh, hi," Joe responded, feeling like he was waking up from a dream.

For a few moments, he just stared at the smiling new friend. He was able to assess that George felt like a life-long acquaintance, even though they had only known each other briefly. Joe had time to process the man's stature. He was slightly older, a timeless creature with a beard that was kept just enough to remain presentable but not overtly pretentious. His eyes were deep and caring and his face worn, but gentle. Everything about his posture was open and receiving, and his clothing blended into the background of the library.

"The last time I saw you, we were determined to discover the reason for your journey," George said, altering the course of the discussion before it began.

What is it about middle-aged men that divert necessary conversation to discussions about the weather and sports and other things that don't usually prove life-changing? George knew that Joe was at a crossroad of sorts, and everything about him suggested he had some answers. Joe could sense George as a mystic guide, but that was about all he could gather at this point.

"I thought a lot about your questions," Joe began. "For hours, I contemplated different aspects of this journey. I kept asking myself the same questions, but I didn't just get one answer; I got many. Like a flood of thoughts that later trickled down into a concise list of valuable takeaways and more questions that might be helpful."

"Mm … yeah," was all that George said, but Joe found it oddly comforting.

"That short list of observations and questions was what I was thinking about while I was waiting for you to come back."

"Oh, I'm sorry to have kept you waiting. I got tied up in another conversation down the road."

"No worries," Joe continued. "It gave me time to sort through my list. I thought about what is important, and about being versus doing, and about urgency and importance. Some of these things are things that I have been wrestling with for years that are becoming clearer, and I feel at least somewhat enlightened about them. They are all a part of the why, but maybe not the primary reason for me to go on this journey to discover whatever it is I am trying to discover. They may be subtexts, but not the topic sentence, know what I mean?"

"I know exactly what you mean!"

George motioned for Joe to continue and took a deep breath like he was focusing all his energy on Joe—like he was peering into his soul. Not in any way to judge what may be said or wait to give rehearsed advice. It was as if he readied himself to absorb both the heart of the speaker and the inclination of the Divine. It was a practical version of namaste that communicated respect and the message, *I'm listening to you!*

"Here's what I think it is," Joe paused and took the deepest breath he had taken in weeks.

When he breathed out, he felt like everything in his mind was melting down and flushing down toward his feet. He could feel himself opening up. His mind was almost clear, his body relaxed, and his surroundings supported and grounded him. He was prepared to speak the truth, and he was at peace.

"Since the first time I stepped into the hotel, I have felt that there are a lot of parallels between the life of the hotel and my own personal life. It is a metaphor in a way or maybe it's an object lesson; I don't actually know. But what I do know is that the things that are hidden or secret are much like the hidden and the secret things in my life. I suspect that there are parts of this story that will help me understand my story. I feel the connection, but I can't understand the significance—at least, not yet."

"So. You feel a connection," George responded, "to the hotel or something you don't yet know about the hotel?"

"Yes, and it's not necessarily what I have discovered or uncovered. I get the sense that it is what I don't yet know that is the connection that causes me to keep moving forward. For so long I feared anything mysterious or untouchable or anything that involved deep feelings. I feel that there is something at the hotel, and something within me that needs to be heard."

"So, something in you needs to be heard," George said, and then he groaned softly, "Mmm … yes!"

"What do you think that means?" Joe questioned, trying to regain his rationality.

"May I suggest, for now, not to try and analyze what you are feeling. Let's return to that feeling you had. If you could describe that feeling, that *something* in you that needs to be heard, how would you describe it? Close your eyes and try to get a sense of what that feeling is."

Joe gazed up at the man he was beginning to trust. He didn't know why, but it felt secure, and he slowly closed his eyes and went through a body scan starting at the top of his head and moving slowly toward his toes. Since he was focused on what matters most, what is important and just being, taking his time. With every breath, he gained more clarity, and then he felt it.

"Yeah—uh—I feel anxious," Joe said as tears formed in his eyes.

"Try this language, Joe," George suggested, "A part of me feels … just like you did before.

"A part of me feels anxious," Joe said confidently, and then he began to cry.

Suddenly, he knew he was communing with something deep within. He didn't feel the need to change it, but he realized it was only a piece of himself. In the past, this might have felt threatening or out of control, but this time he felt mostly just compassion for the part of himself that felt anxious.

"Just be with that part of you," George instructed. "Just be present and sit with it for a while, can you do that?"

Joe nodded his head slowly. He was aware that he occasionally would respond to what he was feeling, but he didn't remember anything he said or did for the time that passed. After about ten minutes, George spoke up.

"Maybe, for now, you would just like to thank the part that communicated with you," George offered humbly, "and give it permission to be or stay as long as necessary."

This seemed a little awkward to Joe, but he essentially said *goodbye* to a part of him and thanked it for communicating with him. After a couple of minutes, his eyes fluttered open, and he saw George's face directly in front of him. They both smiled together, and Joe realized what he felt most was peace.

"What do you feel now?"

"It's hard to explain," Joe said, "but it feels like everything shifted and feels more open and it's lighter."

"That's great!"

They just both nodded their heads and stared at each other for a minute or two, then George explained.

"What you experienced was what some people call *focusing*. You were able to communicate, or feel, a part of you that was most likely stuck. Because you felt this part of you, it is likely that this part of you shifted and will be different because you treated it with compassion. It may take you a long time to think about it, but what you felt was understood."

"That was awesome and different," Joe whispered. "I don't understand, but I love it!"

"That's so awesome! One of the pioneers of focusing, Eugene Gendlin, said, 'What is split off, not felt, remains the same. When it is felt, it changes. Most people don't know this! They think that by not permitting the feeling of their negative ways they make themselves good. On the contrary, that keeps these negatives static, the same from year to year. A few moments of feeling it in your body allows it to change. If there is in you something bad or sick or unsound, let it inwardly be and breathe. That's the only way it can evolve and change into the form it needs.'"

"We store things in our body when we push things down. Some people call it *shadow*. Those things don't go away, but as Gendlin stresses, when we ignore them, they never get better. It is only when we *feel* them that they can evolve and change. It's probably a very deep part of what you are searching for. We could talk more, but it's late, and I must get going."

Joe glanced at his phone and realized they had been here for over an hour. It felt like minutes. *How strange.* Once, he had labored to be silent for ten minutes during contemplative prayer.

"Oh, yeah, I need to be going, too," Joe said, straightening his mask and standing up.

They embraced deeply. Joe couldn't begin to explain his current state, but he understood that he was different because of the encounter. He wondered when the librarian had left, but he relinquished all that to George to handle and hurried home. He was almost glad that Mary was asleep because he would not be able to explain this for a while.

He quickly fell into a deep slumber, but arose early, writing feverishly to try to get all whatever *this* was out.

This would be remembered as a fork in the road where his life began to change. Just like the hotel, he knew he wasn't finished exploring; but for once, he knew he was on the right track.

JUNE 1929—TROUBLE
ON THE HORIZON

"DOES IT SEEM LIKE BUSINESS IS SLOWING DOWN?" ALESA
asked.

"I just noticed that today, and Nancy said we have 5 empty rooms
tonight."

"It is strange for the summer that we are not turning people away.
In a way, it's nice because the load is a little less on everyone, but they
worry something has gone wrong."

"You are the chief worry wart for both of us, but I'm thankful,"
George said gratefully.

"The truth is we are in excellent shape. Our debts are all paid, we
have lots of money in savings, and every investment we've made is
paying off. Also, I'm thankful for our relationship with J.D. All those
partnerships have turned out for the best. I still don't know where
he came up with some of the *resources* he finds. I'm grateful, but it's
a little suspicious. I could say the same about many of the people in
town."

Alesa had been waiting to talk for a while, and she sat down,
appearing satisfied. There is no doubt her parents were demanding,
and she certainly lived with that unfinished business of never feeling
like she could accomplish enough. But J.D. and George were helping
her make those dreams come true. Everything they were doing during
this decade was coming up roses, and she didn't mind being the brains
and the conscious and the energy for making it work. It was obvious
that she was the real *boss,* but in those times, you didn't admit that.
Today, her face told the story that she knew her value.

"We have had a good run," George announced, "and I can't wait to see what is next. I wish the rest of my family would celebrate with us. The last time I talked to dad, he asked me when I'm going to stop this foolishness and just come work on the farm. He worked so hard to make the farm go, and now he wants me to continue. I wish he would just sell out and move to town, but to guys like him, the town is a den of iniquity."

"Speaking of iniquity, have you seen the busybodies lately?" Alesa questioned. "I haven't seen them around. I know we haven't got any more perfect, so I'm sure they are still dissatisfied with whatever we are doing wrong."

"I heard they had a meeting with what's his name at the lumberyard." George said. "It's the whole morality, temperance, holier-than-everyone group that gets all fired up every so often. I heard they are trying to get organized to do some kind of march."

"Against whom?"

"Against us, I guess!" George continued. "It's perplexing, most of them have never been inside the hotel, but they have an opinion of what happens here. I remember my dad doing that at home. His only points of reference were the couple of times he came to town at night and his vivid imagination. They all don't have enough to do, and they just get each other riled up."

"Well, if the leader of the old hens comes in here again, "Alesa continued, "I'm going to challenge her to a duel."

"A duel?"

"Well, what do you call it when two women fight?"

"Some people call it a cat fight," George explained, "but if you fought with that particular old hen, it would probably be called an *ass whippin'*!"

"I don't know what people want. Sometimes, I think they want everyone to be as miserable as them. You can never please them totally.

Hey ... speak of the devil, there they are. What are they doing across the street? They are writing something down."

George stepped out on the porch and addressed the ladies and an unidentified man, "Hey what are you writing down?"

The group scurried off, like a pack of mice that had been discovered.

"They were writing down license plates," Ricky said coming out of the kitchen. "They think you guys are selling liquor illegally, so they're going to call those license plates into the state guys in the city. I was in the bank the other day and heard them talking, but I just now put the pieces together of what they were talking about. Most of them have never been into the restaurant and didn't know who I was."

Alesa gave the look. She was losing her temper. She'd always turned her head to the side and started for the door with a determined gate. Luckily, George intercepted her and was able to slow her down long enough for the emotion to pass and for them to regain composure.

"Listen up everyone, gather up." George began, "You have all worked hard to make this place the best hotel in a hundred miles. It's the place to be! We appreciate all of you, but people like the ladies across the street, who don't have enough to mess with, will try to sabotage what we are doing. In their minds, we're having orgies and all kinds of things here, but you know different. Please try never to respond to accusations from them—they just want you to react and do something silly."

Nobody verbally responded, but they all nodded in agreement. George didn't speak that often, so when he did, they listened to each carefully selected word, and they absorbed it. They knew Alesa would answer questions later if there were any.

The phone rang, giving them all a chance to return to work. The 1920s boom had been prosperous for them. They each knew their jobs and loved making it happen every day. It was a predictable cycle of activity that happened rhythmically, but there were also the twists and turns and the unexpected nature of having different people there every day. They loved their work, and they loved the Poppers.

"Hello J.D.," Nancy said. "Sure, I'll get George."

Nancy handed the phone to George. Alesa still resented it a little that she was never considered *the boss* or an equal partner. It wasn't a matter of disrespect; it was just prejudices of the times. Women had gained the right to vote, but they were still fighting to be heard and accepted. In a way, it was what the busybodies were doing as well.

"J.D., what's up? When are you coming to see us again?"

"Very soon. I'll let Nancy know the dates. We have a couple of meetings scheduled, and I have someone I would like you to meet. He's a politician, but I'm backing him here in the city. He could be the president someday! But that's not why I called."

"So, what can we do for you?"

"I have a half-brother, Phillip. He is tired of the city and would love to get out of the rat race. He owns a car dealership and would love to move it to a smaller venue. You don't have a good car dealership around there, right? I know you don't. But also, my friend from up North says there is some land that was recently flooded near you that is for sale dirt cheap."

"Why should that interest us?" George asked, knowing that whatever J.D. was planning, he had most of it already in motion and just needed an agreement from the Poppers to set his mind at ease.

"That's the beauty of this whole thing," J.D. charged ahead. "There are people from the city that would pay a lot of money to watch the migratory birds come in. With a little work, that flooded land could become an invite-only paradise for people with too much money. The fortunate thing about Phillip is he also knows land-development. He can do both ventures, and you and I can split the profits with him. It's a win-win!"

"That does sound interesting," George continued, "but you know, we need to talk to Alesa."

"Have her call me when she gets free. I'm heading out the door, but I'll be back. Give me two hours."

Exactly two hours later, his phone rang, and Alesa was on the other end of the line. George assessed that she had a hundred questions for him, but she emerged from the discussion with a smile on her face. George didn't even ask, but knew that all was well, and he assumed Phillip was already in town somewhere waiting for the go-ahead from J.D. Only weeks later, construction began on Ideal Motors, and George wondered to himself why no one told him Phillip was a little crazy. It wouldn't have been as bad, but the dealership was right across the street.

Phillip mostly kept to himself, which was okay with George, but it bothered Alesa somewhat. He didn't sell many cars, but he was making great progress on the bird sanctuary. The basin was perfect for the ten acres of marshland that naturally expanded into a small lake at its deepest end. . It was directly aligned with migration paths of geese, ducks, and other waterfowl. Lyle helped build the modest but luxurious cottages that speckled the water's edge. They were conveniently made to withstand any flooding for those escaping not only the city, but also the elements.

When George did his rounds that morning, something felt different. There wasn't hardly anyone on the streets, but people were huddling to discuss something. In a small town, this could be that someone died or that the busybodies had stirred everyone up. He wasn't even nervous about it anymore, but figured, eventually, the gossip would make its way to the restaurant. He usually didn't wade into the murky waters of the café down the street, knowing that at the least, it meant he would have to have way too much meaningless conversation.

As he entered the hotel, he noticed almost everyone in the hotel was gathered around the radio in the parlor. Radio was a key means of entertainment for the hotel, and at certain times of the day, Nancy would turn it up and invite guests to gather around and enjoy the show. But this was an unusual time for them to be gathering at all, and it sounded more like a news broadcast than a show. They usually didn't listen to the news because the guests were trying to get away, but obviously this was something important.

Before he could even hear it, Ricky met him near the door, "The stock market is crashing!"

George didn't even know exactly what that meant. But he didn't want to sit around and listen to the cackle about something they didn't understand either. So, instead of joining in the chaos, he snatched up a newspaper and headed down to his sanctuary beneath the hotel. Alesa knew to gather the facts and just give him the summary—that was enough for him.

When she finally came down, George closed the paper and said softly, "This is something big, isn't it?"

She didn't say anything, just nodded and embraced him. After a few seconds, they clasped hands and walked back upstairs to assess things. For most of the rest of the day, nobody said anything. The hotel was close to empty that night and nobody knew what to say.

J.D., CRAZY PHILLIP, AND HIS WEIRD OBSESSION

"FOR THE FIRST TIME IN A FEW WEEKS, I THINK I'M excited," Alesa blurted out. "It's been kind of dead, and J.D. always livens up the place."

"Indeed. You want some breakfast?" George offered.

Ricky was one step ahead of them and was already headed back to the conference room with their favorite breakfast. He served them like they were first time customers, even though, by now, they were the best of friends and none of those formalities were necessary.

"You know small town people have a way of surviving this type of downturn," Ricky said, still poised like a waiter ready to serve them.

"Indeed, they do," George said, pausing only briefly from his breakfast to put in the only two cents he was going to give.

"It's a little more than a downturn," Alesa began. "It's going to make its way to us. In fact, it already has. We haven't been half full in weeks. It will most likely get worse before it gets better. But you are right, in small towns, people *put up* vegetables and have supplies of all kinds stored up. They already know how to live on a little less, and they can just stay home and wait it out. I think it's also true that people out here on the plains, essentially, can still remember that it wasn't that long ago that none of this was here, and they can still walk out in their backyard and spend the night looking at the stars."

"We just want you to know," George added, "the hotel is going to be okay. We may have to bail the bank out, but we're okay!"

"I appreciate that," Ricky said, "but no one can predict the future. But, if I have to go under with anyone, I'll do it with you guys. If we all have to come live here, just don't let that Phillip character in—he's kind of nutty. By the way, what's he doing with all that dirt?"

"I don't know. I hesitate to even go over there," George said.

"I need to give him something later," Alesa said. "I'll ask him. Maybe it's something for the sanctuary."

Just like they usually did, everyone just went back to their duties. There was a rhythm and heartbeat about the whole operation that made it easier to get things done. Everyone knew their responsibilities and expectations, and there wasn't any competition because Alesa didn't allow it. Especially during these leaner times, there was no time wasted on drama or gameplay. Everyone understood their job and did it.

Some of them volunteered at the soup line Alesa had opened once a day for those that couldn't afford the restaurant's food. Occasionally someone would ask for help, and they always had a little something in the can that someone more fortunate had given them.

They were busy when J.D. arrived. The staff knew not to over dramatize his arrival but made him feel welcome just the same. He asked Nancy to book him for the night, and she went to prepare the best room (a double) for him and anyone that might tag along.

"There will be a couple of men arriving shortly, just give them their own room, and we'll figure out later who is staying and who is going back."

"Hello, J.D.," Alesa said as the couple arrived from the back of the hotel.

"Hello, friends," J.D. answered as he paused to look at them lovingly and drew close for a hug. "We need to get right down to business. We have a lot to talk about. How is Phillip working out?"

"He's doing fine, I think," George said. "He did a fabulous job creating the sanctuary. It's almost done, and we could take a tour later.

I'm not sure he has sold any cars, but he gets quite a lot of repair work. You forgot to tell us that he was crazy!"

"He's not crazy. He's just eccentric. He's very smart, and he just never fits in that well. You can relate to that, can't you George?"

"I guess so," George responded.

"First thing on the agenda is something you may not be aware of," J.D. continued, "and it involves the aforementioned Phillip. You see, he has this brilliant idea. To save money with some landfill, he started digging underneath the town."

"What do you mean," Alesa interrupted, "like tunnels?"

"Exactly like tunnels. You see, Phillip is kind of like me. He always has a couple of ideas that get combined. So, he needed free dirt, and he also wanted to have some free storage underground, like a cellar. It's temperature controlled and all that. Again, George, you should be able to relate to that, right?"

"Well, yeah, I guess that's right"

"Well, here's where it gets interesting. So, one of the tunnels, or extended basement if you please, goes directly under the street and is now approximately 3 feet from your wine cellar."

"Wait a minute," Alesa interjected again. "I see where this is going. You want us to give crazy Phillip access to our property? Isn't that a little risky? No offense, he is likely a harmless guy, but I don't know if I want him spelunking underneath me at night while I'm trying to go to sleep. And how did he move all the dirt without the busybodies finding him out?"

J.D. looked at George like he thought about telling her to be quiet, like he would have in times past, but when she leaned closer and made eye contact, he knew the best course of action would be to talk to her directly and respect the fact that she wanted her questions answered.

"Phillip's idea is this: to take the pressure off you guys, customers buying alcohol could come through the tunnel instead of entering through the front door. If they came to the auto dealership, they would just look like customers, and no one would suspect them of buying liquor. George, you, and Phillip should talk. In many ways you think alike, and I think you guys could come up with a speakeasy or some kind of place that was away from prying eyes."

"But no one is spending money!" Alesa countered.

"I know, but while we are not so busy, some of that can be arranged and made ready. Then, when the economy comes back, we will be all set! I'm in for half the cost for half the profit."

"We will talk about it," George said, looking at Alesa.

"Number two," J.D. announced without missing a beat, "is we need to buy farmland."

"Wait, a minute," George objected. "We're trying to get out of the farming business for now."

"No, I don't mean we need to farm. But we can buy farmland dirt cheap. When the economy comes back, we can rent it out to farmers. I know you want to get your parents off their farm and help them retire. You could buy them out and snatch up some other land to rent out when things get better. It's a buyer's market, as they say!"

"That totally makes sense, but we'll have to think it over," Alesa said forcefully, "no snap decisions here. We don't have unlimited resources. And we don't know what is going to happen."

"I get it," J.D. said, "but it won't last forever."

"Let's go out and see Phillip," George said.

Like a gang of children, they all jumped up and headed for the door.

They spent the remainder of the day relaxing at the bird sanctuary. It was amazing what the guys had accomplished in a short amount of time. The cabins were simply perfect for small gatherings and a club-house had been added off the main road for venues and gatherings of larger groups. The tributaries that fed the lake and the nearby river were visible in two directions and the marsh provided beautiful and peaceful visions of feathered visitors.

At random times during the afternoon, someone could be found asleep sitting against a rail or wherever there was a pleasant view to observe. It felt comforting not having anywhere to be or anything that was expected of them. They were so relaxed that they never even saw the sheriff drive up the long entryway.

"George. Alesa. And you must be J.D." The sheriff reached out to shake the hand of the businessman. "You do a lot of business in this area; how come I haven't ever met you before?"

The sheriff looked hard into the eyes of the city businessman. J.D. held his gaze, but then peered down with a look that the couple had never seen before. He became a little more realistic and answered less directly.

"I'm just a busy man, sheriff."

"You and George are going to own everything soon!"

"Don't forget about me," Alesa chimed in.

"There's no crime in investing, is there sheriff?" J.D. spoke slowly this time and directly.

"No sir, there sure isn't," the sheriff said, chuckling to himself. "Just keep your head above water where I can see you, right?"

"You got it, sir!"

"Good day, folks," the sheriff said walking away.

"I'm not a fan," Alesa said, almost loud enough for the sheriff to hear.

"Big fish in a small pond," J.D. said. "You can't fault him for trying to do the right thing. No one ever told him how to be polite; they just told him he's in charge, and he is probably a little insecure inside. Most county sheriffs are honorable, decent people, but power corrupts, and absolute power corrupts absolutely as they say. They are kind of like pastors in a way, when you tell them they have *authority*, it goes to their head."

"Indeed," George said simply, hoping to derail the conversation, so they could get back to the hotel.

"It's probably all that chirping those dames downtown have been doing in his ear that got him to follow us out here," said Alesa. "You'd think with the depression and all that they could find something productive to do."

They all kind of shook their heads and headed back. Everyone was tired from the day and ready to have a hearty meal. *Surely Ricky will make something special since J.D. is here*, George thought to himself. The wheels were turning for all of them. Success often breeds success, but they were in an interesting time. For the people that hadn't overspent in the prosperous times, there were lots of opportunities to buy low for profit later.

"They're back," Nancy yelled as they walked up the steps. "Ricky made some dinner, it's just about ready. You guys can just be comfortable if you want. A few of the guests are listening to some news on the radio. It's a little scary, but we might as well know what's going on."

They listened for a while, but when they caught a glimpse of food, it got the better of them, and they ate like hungry children for a few minutes before anyone spoke up.

"We need to give more to the community," J.D. said, looking up from his meal.

"Oh, yeah?" George responded. "What do you mean by that?"

"So many people are suffering. We can't save them all, and some of them deserve to be down, but we can help many of them that can't help themselves. Some day when this is over, I think they will remember who helped them and who didn't. That may sound selfish, but it's also the right thing to do if I remember right from when I went to church back in the day."

They all just shook their heads and kept eating.

After limited conversation, Alesa went to finish paperwork, and George brought up a bottle of wine to drink with J.D. They enjoyed their glasses in silence until J.D. finally broke in.

"You know you're going to have to let it out eventually," J.D. began.

"Oh, let what out?" George deflected.

"I'm sorry for springing that on you, but that's what I had to do with the things that troubled me from my past," J.D. began. "That time when you saw me crying ... Well, part of that was motivated by some philosophers I was reading at the time. The trouble with pushing things down is that it doesn't stay down there. Have you ever just blown up at Alesa for seemingly no reason?"

"Of course, I have, that's fairly normal—"

J.D. continued without waiting for George to finish, "It may be "normal," but maybe you would agree it's not helpful. You also feel bad after it happens, right? And then you can't explain why it happens. Something just happens and then you react in the most unhelpful ways. I have found, through some of these philosophies, that if I spend some time feeling what I don't want to feel, somehow it gets better, and I don't react as much. For example, today when the sheriff was accusing me of something without even knowing me, I was able to breathe through it and respond responsibly."

"But we have a saying around here," George explained, hoping to derail this. "Let sleeping dogs lie."

"The trouble with that," J.D. interrupted, "is the dogs don't stay asleep and sometimes they come back to bite you."

George glared at J.D. for what seemed like 5 minutes. His eyes were filled with tears, and he felt like at any time, he would burst out in a rage. He couldn't imagine striking his friend, but he wanted him to just drop it like he had a thousand times. But the trouble was that J.D. was right. It didn't get any better. He couldn't even have a conversation with his own father, and every time something reminded him of his childhood, he reacted in the worst way.

"So, what can I do?" he said, hanging his head. He wanted to cry but he couldn't.

"Will you let me help you, George?"

George got up and locked the outer door to the conference room. He walked around the room a couple of times before he came back and sat down. He looked at J.D. He glanced up at the ceiling, and then he stared back at his friend.

"Okay, tell me what to do."

"Why don't you start by telling me about you and your dad?" J.D. began. "It's obvious that you guys can't communicate with each other after all this time. What was it like growing up with him?"

George shook his head a few times until his eyes filled with tears.

"What did it feel like, tell me everything!" J.D. prompted. "Where do you feel it now?"

George began talking and didn't stop for twenty minutes. He told J.D. every single detail. At times, he would pace around the room. At other times, he would slap his hand on the table and swear and wave his arms. He talked about the look of consternation on his father's face and what happened when George disappointed him.

J.D. listened with a compassion George had never seen except times when Alesa listened to him. J.D. shook his head and urged George to continue, but he never stopped George except to ask clarifying questions when the answer was too vague. He mainly just listened.

When George finished, he collapsed on the table, exhausted and sobbing from the weight of what he had shared. After a couple of minutes, J.D. spoke up.

"Thank you for sharing that with me," J.D. said. "Now, what do you feel and where do you feel it?"

"Right here," George said, pointing to his heart. "I feel anger; I feel sadness." Then he gasped and said, "I feel rejected! I feel rejected, dammit! I feel rejected!"

His arms were open, like he had just discovered something, and he simply wept for a minute or so before he looked to J.D. who, too, was teary-eyed and simply nodding his head saying, "Yeah, yeah, you found it. You found where you are stuck."

For the next few minutes, George was quiet, then turning his head to the side, he said, "Umm…it feels like something changed. I feel more open! I feel lighter. What happened?"

"I don't know how to explain it," J.D. offered, "but it's the same thing that happened to me."

"What kind of voodoo are you doing to me?" George teased as they both chuckled together.

J.D. couldn't take it any longer and walked around the table to hug his younger friend. They were both exhausted, so with a nod to each other, they parted without another word and headed off bed. Alesa met him there like she knew, but she didn't say anything. She just held him and peered into his eyes.

"Let's talk in the morning," he said, and she nestled against his side as he drifted to sleep.

THE CRASH

THEY DIDN'T GET TO TALK IN THE MORNING BECAUSE George slept in. As he finally stumbled out into the busy activity of the hotel, he normally would have received a look from Alesa, but today she beamed with compassion and love. During the time with J.D., he was able to block out everything around him, but Alesa was aware and watching from a distance. She knew everything that happened inside the hotel, including when her husband was struggling.

He winked at her to let her know that he was okay as she helped a customer decipher their bill. The staff wasn't quite as busy anymore, so they started later than usual, knowing there was plenty of time to complete their limited tasks for the day. Some, like Ricky, were as busy as ever since everyone in town struggled to put food on their tables. The interesting thing about this time of crisis was extra ham from a fat, butchered boar or an overabundant garden crop would regularly make its way to the restaurant to be distributed wisely.

During the 1920s in the United States, the economy expanded rapidly. The total wealth in the nation more than doubled. Since people had wealth like never before, they were recklessly speculating in the stock market among other things. But the market peaked towards the end of 1929, and inevitably led to nervous investors dumping millions of stocks until it crashed in October of that year. Investors who bought on margin were wiped out completely, while others were indirectly affected including farmers.

The agricultural areas mainly struggled due to the years of drought that culminated in the Dust Bowl. No one had the money to buy food, so the prices plummeted. Banks couldn't loan money or give credit as loans (especially from farmers) defaulted. Confidence vanished from the marketplace and unemployment skyrocketed. And even as Herbert Hoover encouraged people that the "crisis" would soon run its course, by 1930, 4 million Americans were unemployed, and by 1931, the number had risen to 6 million.

Eventually, harvesting became impossible. Roots shriveled and loosed the soil to run amuck and blow through the homes and hearts and lives of the American farmer. Families left the land in hopes of work in the urban streets and factories. Eventually, banks felt the full weight of the depression and many of them closed their doors as business, temporarily or permanently, stopped operating altogether.

During those days at the hotel, the employees felt like they were just trying to endure. The hotel was usually about half full because some people still had to travel, and this was the place to stay. Travelers were not taking excessive vacations, but often leaders of industry and organizations like J.D. Enterprises still needed a place to stay away from the city and the Hoovervilles. There remained some wealthier guests who retreated from the pressures of the depression, but not as many as before.

After his experience with J.D., George didn't feel like he was totally healed or dramatically changed, but he did feel more aware of what was going on inside himself. So, despite all that was occurring, as pressure arose, or something triggered him, he noticed he was more apt to breath and not react. It was having a significant impact, but it was extremely hard to describe how he had changed.

One Tuesday morning, as most of the staff was staring out the window waiting for something to happen, Alesa pulled George aside like she was going to tell him something important. There was an urgency that worried George a little, but he also noticed a smile. He took just a second to appreciate how beautiful she was. He admired most everything about her and because his insides weren't just reacting anymore, he often saw her a little deeper.

"Okay, hear me out," she began. "I want to propose something."

"Go ahead, I'm listening."

"Okay, we've worked fairly hard for about a decade. We've made this place something spectacular. We will most likely survive this depression because we have avoided the spending that got the country in this situation. We've done everything right, except for one thing."

"What is that?"

"We have never taken a vacation."

As she continued to talk, George thought back through the years. They had never even considered going somewhere else. In many ways, they felt like they were on vacation because they were at the place everyone else wanted to be. Even better, they got paid to be here. In the early days, it was necessary for them to be here since they didn't have the capable staff. But now, deep down, they both knew they could take a vacation. In a way, they just didn't know how.

"But should we spend the money now, during the depression?" George asked.

"That's the beauty of it," she continued. "Now, we own another vacation spot where we can stay for free. The sanctuary has everything we need to totally get away. It's beautiful this time of year, the geese should be arriving soon. I've thought about it for a week, and I can't think of any reason why we shouldn't go. Look at the staff. They are bored because of the drop in business—let's do this!"

"I actually like the idea. This thing … that happened the other day … has changed me."

"Yes!" Alesa said in her best celebration pose. "We're leaving Monday for a week!"

"Hey, let me throw a twist into the mix."

"Okay, but don't be twisting up my plan too much. I have a distinct idea how I want this to go. I already drew up the itinerary and have planned it all out in my mind."

Essentially, it was Alesa's planning and organization that made the hotel and all their other businesses run. Fueled by her dysfunctional upbringing in part, she meticulously planned and executed every detail and took pride in the fact that those plans produced incredible results. Occasionally, the staff felt like the control was overboard, but most times they were thankful for her organized and driven mind. Some days, it reminded George of his father, but he also was grateful for her leadership.

"When we get back," George suggested humbly, "let's give each of our employees a week at the sanctuary. We can afford it during these times. They will appreciate it and all it will cost us is for us to pick up the slack. This may be the only time that this would work."

"That's a genius idea!" she said.

And with that George decided to stop while he was ahead.

Like most days, when the plan was understood, they silently went about getting things ready. George made sure his inventory was in order and made a few notes to give to Ricky. Alesa glanced at the books and also scribbled a few lists for Nancy. They didn't even have to discuss that these two older employees would be in charge. It would cause them to rise up to full business mode, but they could easily handle it and would probably look forward to the challenge.

"What's going on?" Nancy said, inquisitively. "I know something is going on, what is it?"

"We will tell everyone in about an hour. It's great news!"

Nancy had developed, over the years, into a suitable assistant to Alesa. Their personalities were similar, and they essentially mirrored the same job just at various times of the day. It wasn't that they finished each other's sentences; they often didn't even have to talk to know what the other was thinking. George was a little jealous because he and his wife were so polar opposite that they often struggled to communicate even when they were thinking alike.

"Okay, I'll tell you," Alesa blurted out, like a newly engaged teenager.

"Thank you. I was a little hurt that you wouldn't tell ME!"

"George and I have decided to take a vacation, so we're going to the sanctuary for a week!"

"Oh my god, I can't believe that … ," she said. "That's … perfect! Wow!"

Once again, they didn't need to talk. They embraced each other and celebrated like sisters. The idea to take a vacation was so long overdue and so obvious, it was almost like the hotel itself was catching on to the idea and celebrating with them. Alesa breathed deeply as though she was inhaling the depth of her own understanding—this was the right decision. They were gonna make it count.

"Oh, I should … ," Nancy trailed off, realizing she now had some things that needed her attention if Alesa was going to be gone. *I'm going to be Alesa for a week*, she thought to herself. She couldn't help but smile.

It took only five minutes for the entire staff to learn about the vacation. George and Alesa just smiled to themselves when they realized everyone knew. They were family, without secrets, at least from each other.

"Okay, everyone, gather up front," George began, "You already know, so—"

Alesa interrupted, knowing that George wouldn't give enough details. She laid out the responsibilities to everyone and wished them well. Just like with Nancy, it didn't take a lot of convincing, and everyone knew what they needed to do. Everyone was smiling—this was long overdue.

"And one more thing," George added. "When we get back, each of you will get a paid week off at the sanctuary!"

With that, the staff just broke into a celebration! The two days until they left, it was more like everyone was floating on air. Everyone was playful and whistling or singing to themselves. The couple felt like they were traveling across the sea to a foreign land when they left to visit their own property 7.2 miles away!

And for a brief time, no one remembered they were in a depression.

THE SANCTUARY

As they arrived at the sanctuary, the caretaker met them at the door. This was another prudent decision. The couple that basically lived at the sanctuary loved birds and people and seemed to be right at home running the business for little to no money. They had fallen on hard times and needed a place to live. They were warm and friendly and resourceful. Alesa talked to them once a week to keep things straight. The couples exchanged smiles and a quick bit of small talk as Ed and Martha gathered their bags and walked to the luxury cabin.

George stopped for a second to listen to the radio in the lobby. The hosts were talking about the presidential candidates. George was interested because he heard much about both, but more focused on what Roosevelt planned for the economy. Politics made him think about his father who was always ranting about one thing or another. George hadn't ever had the time to sit at the café and discuss such things but a part of him wanted to.

Alesa caught him by the arm and dragged him away. Their gait was that of newlyweds again. Alesa was near to skipping as they looked up, hearing a small gaggle of geese making their way across the afternoon sky. This was the right decision. The room was perfectly set up with a few extras like fresh flowers and local fruits that Alesa had arranged to be delivered.

"You're all set," Martha said. "You know more than us about this room, so ... "

Her voice trailed off with a wink as they backed out of the room, a little nervous that their owners were now their customers. They disappeared into the misty afternoon stillness as the hotel owners looked at each other, their eyes widening, then both smiling at the bed. George lifted his wife high in the air, then slowly lowered her along his torso until she wrapped her legs tightly around his waist. His mind flashed back to their small house in the country as she kissed him. They fell back in the bed, tearing at each other's clothes and groaning passionately. Alesa glanced up only to make sure the curtains were closed and then pulled him close once again.

The rest of the night was more of the same. They would sip wine and stargaze only to return to the bedroom and take up where they'd left off. They didn't talk about anything in particular, just occasionally saying to themselves, *this is great!*

It was a bit awkward adjusting to the privacy and the quiet. George toyed with the idea of going up to the lobby but thought better of it and realized they were going to both have to relish this quieter mode of being.

He stood outside for almost an hour shortly after midnight. Alesa had fallen asleep, and he took the chance to remember some star formations he learned about in school. The boys had arranged the lighting strategically where you could still walk along the wooden planks safely, but it still appeared totally dark when you one would look up at the stars. It faintly reminded him of the farm, so he struggled to make sense of everything—his loves, his fears, and his trauma. Occasionally he would take a deep breath and close his eyes to focus deeper, but his mind still also raced with the cares he recently abandoned.

Beyond his view, George could hear the symphony of bullfrogs and crickets and the occasional yelp of the coyotes coming out to scavenge. He knew not to be afraid, because most of the animals would never come close to humans unless they were forced to do so. The sounds of nature always sounded like they had a rhythm and a cadence that was hard to explain. It comforted him in times when he was alone and gave him courage that there was a purpose to everything. In a way, it was how he experienced what he knew as God.

When the symphony paused, he heard her sobbing and returned to the room.

"What's wrong babe?" he said softly, hoping it was just a bad dream.

"It's just the same old stuff," she said between sniffles and more tears.

"Would you like to talk about it?" George said softly.

"You know, I listened when J.D. talked to you that night. I've heard some city guests talking about "shadow" philosophy, and how it works. It's just that my past is so complicated, and I don't think you know everything about it. My dad, my mom, and the other incident that nobody knows about."

"The other incident?"

"Maybe, I can do this. Will you listen to me? I need to get this out!"

"Absolutely," George said.

"Okay, just sit over there and listen!"

"Okay, I'm ready. Do you need a drink?"

"Just water and please close the blinds."

Alesa stared at the picture on the wall. She didn't realize it earlier, but it was a picture of her parents' homestead. She had donated it to the sanctuary because she didn't want it around the hotel every day, but she did not want to throw it away. It caught her eye this evening, and it transported her back to her childhood and her days on the old homestead. For the most part, they were joyful times, but parts of her experience there had affected her.

"Okay, please promise not to give me any advice. Do not judge. Just listen, okay?"

"I won't ... I mean I promise."

She chuckled a little, knowing that was pure George to be a little nervous about what to say, but she was optimistic that because of his encounter with J.D. he might be able to help her. This was going to be hard, but generally she thrived by facing her fears. This was going to be a new adventure and somewhere during the night she convinced herself it was worth pursuing.

"I remember that it was never okay to show emotion around my home. You know I was an only child. Once when I was five, our teacher told us she had cancer, I came home crying and my mother scolded me. She told me that we didn't have time for tears and ordered me outside to do my chores. Everything in me wanted to just cry and feel sorry for the teacher, but I couldn't. I was afraid my mom would smack me, and her response was so abrupt, that something in me shut down until I could actually watch animals die on the farm without shedding a tear. I sensed my mom was proud of me for being mature, so something inside me just got stuck there. Whenever, I start to feel something sad or hurtful, I often just shut down and would go do my *chores* for the day ... "

She trailed off a little then sort of gasped and began to cry again.

"Aww ... Yes, you were sad, you wanted to be sad ... " he offered.

She nodded her head and continued.

"We've talked about this a little and you know this. But my parents were very demanding. They were the children of immigrants, and they wanted us all to have a better life. They only knew how to work, and so they channeled all their hopes and dreams into their work and into me. From the time I could carry objects I was working and performing. Every time I presented them with my accomplishment, they would only suggest how it could be better. I learned never to celebrate my accomplishments, but only to keep working to make them better. It wasn't until I met you, that I heard a genuine compliment from someone close to me."

"So, you felt like part of you was stuck there also trying to find approval?"

"Yes, and it didn't matter how many awards I won, it was never enough because a part of me felt unacceptable, still trying to find approval and reach some unattainable goal. It has been satisfying to find success at the hotel and learn to accept praise from others, but part of me is still stuck on the farm ... on THAT farm ... "

She trailed off again as she breathed deep, almost struggling for air as wept again. She was feeling everything she felt as a five-year-old child.

"The other thing is going to have to wait until later ... I can't right now."

"That's okay, Babe, just feel what you are feeling. Be with that five-year-old image of yourself. I know it's painful, but I think you are supposed to stay with her."

"I will," she said softly. "I will."

Alesa closed her eyes tightly and made a sound that George remembered from his visit with J.D. On the exterior, it sounded like *oh, God*, but it was more like a groan that he was releasing something. J.D. explained it as feeling like a new birth that was somewhat painful but also like a new life.

"I got you, I got you," she said over and over. "You're good enough ... You ARE enough!"

Then she was shouting, but he couldn't envision a more compassionate display of emotion. She was reaching out to a part of her that had never experienced this level of acceptance and concern before. She was still crying, but she was as intentional as he had ever seen her.

"I got you, you're going to be okay," she said as she rolled on the bed hugging an invisible image of ... herself.

George could only smile and say to himself, *Yes!*

When her body relaxed and her breathing calmed, George pulled back the covers and tucked them both in. They fell asleep in each other's arms, but this time they did talk about it in the morning.

"It's no wonder that I'm so hard on myself and have ulcers. I never realized that there was a part of me that felt that ... that pain ... that rejection. Until I let myself actually feel it, it was going to stay stuck."

"Exactly," George said. "That's how it works. If we try not to feel it, it is like it just roots down deeper inside us, and for me, then it comes out sideways later."

"Me too, but now ... now I feel like it was released. I still hear my parent's words, but that part of me is not stuck in that tiny school-room anymore. I'll probably always have a strong personality, but I don't feel handcuffed by it any longer. This is so amazing!"

"I'm so proud of you!" George said, reverting to the man of few words she loved so dearly.

"Thank you, I believe I can finally accept those words. I feel like this is the start of something new. I know there are other things. There is one thing that is gigantic, but I think I need a different setting and I don't know if I could take another night like that ...not yet anyway."

"We've got the rest of our lives, Babe."

"Indeed, we do!"

They toasted to beginnings and spent the rest of their vacation try-ing to walk on new legs. They received several messages while they were there, but none of them seemed important and only caused them to think about ways they could help those people. George finally opened up to Alesa about another plan, and she listened like she always did.

"I've got an idea for the soup line," George said as they were leav-ing. "I'll tell you when we get back."

THE SOUP KITCHEN

THE COUPLE INTENTIONALLY ARRIVED BACK AT THE hotel at a specific time of night where they would only have to see a few staff. As they walked in, Nancy was gathering up to leave. They quickly said hello and goodbye to her (the girls hugging in between giggles) and went directly to their apartment. After a good night's sleep, they woke up early, anxious to get back to work and routine, although both of them felt like they had a different tool set to work with after the therapeutic week.

George didn't say anything but walked past the newspaper and left to see Phillip. He wasn't sure he would be awake yet and was surprised to see the unusual man seated outside of the car dealership with coffee in hand sitting on a metal chair.

"Hey, George!"

"Hey, Phillip!"

"What are you doing slumming over on this side of town?" he laughed.

"Hey, would you be willing to discuss an idea with me and Alesa?"

"Fix me some breakfast and you got a deal!" Phillip said.

George at times sensed what people said was true about Phillip. He may very well be smart, but he was so socially awkward at times. However, his business was doing well, and he was liked by the community, so George tended to keep his distance and let him do his thing.

The couple forgot how much they missed Ricky's cooking. Phillip inhaled his first plate and didn't start talking until he was well into his second helping of everything.

"So, what did you guys want to talk to me about? I need to go grocery shopping and I want to listen to my show on the radio before the shop opens."

"Wait a minute!" George interrupted. "Why are you acting normal?"

"You don't know," Phillip said smiling.

"I know," Alesa said as George appeared perplexed.

"It's all an act, dude," Phillip said laughing out loud. "You didn't know."

"It is so people won't bother him," Alesa explained, "at least certain people."

George still seemed perplexed. He was running through past conversations in his mind and Alesa and Phillip felt content just to smile at him as he tried to understand the revelation.

"Let me explain a little better. When certain people (like those busybody ladies) are around, if I act crazy, they don't come around very often, and they don't invite me to church. The sheriff thinks I'm crazy, so he doesn't poke around too much, even though I'm not doing anything wrong. It's easier to control the *traffic* in my life. I get sensory overload and most of the time I just want to be by myself."

"But you acted crazy around me," George calculated, "but not around … her?"

Phillip was standing up, so he just curtsied and left the room to get some more breakfast.

"Wait, you guys aren't having an affair, are you?

"Don't be ridiculous!" Alesa scolded, "We need to get this discussion wrapped up soon!"

"Okay," George began as Phillip returned, "let's get back on topic Mr. Crazy Phillip and Mrs. Liar. I want to expand the soup line to be a soup kitchen. Since the restaurant has enough to do, I want to divert that traffic somewhere else and expand what we do. Your shop,

Crazy Phillip, has that whole side that is not being used. I know it's the entrance to the tunnel, but we can cover that up."

Phillip started to interrupt, but George held his hand up like he wanted to finish.

"We can do more than just hand out soup once a day. If this depression continues, it's only going to get worse for people, and they will need food more often. It's also getting cold, and people need coats and gloves and such. People need one place to go for these things and one place to donate if they have extra. It could be like the clearinghouse for all things charity."

"Do we have to pay for staff?" Alesa said in her business voice.

"No, that's the beauty of it. We can get the other charity groups in town who don't know what to do to take turns volunteering there. It won't be too much of a burden on anyone and don't worry about the busybodies. Their church and their friends will insist on doing their own thing, even though it will never work since they are outside of town."

"Two birds with one stone," Phillip said in his crazy voice.

"Phillip, after a while, we can also do alcohol sales from the same counter where we distribute necessities. You can package it like the care packages you hand out and those that care will never be the wiser. Just pass the word that alcohol sales are at specific times, and we should be fine. Do it when the volunteers aren't working and lock the door to the tunnel."

"It's a solid plan, but it needs some more levels of safeguards," Phillip said academically.

"Obviously," Alesa said.

"Are you guys on some kind of new team against me?" George questioned.

"No, but we'll meet at our regular time and iron out all the details," Alesa said confidently. "I think there are a few older ladies in town that are friends with Nancy that have been looking for something like this, and they'll work for free. They don't care about the alcohol, so they'll keep that secret. I can't wait to work on this!"

"Thanks for your enthusiasm," George said. "You in, Phillip?"

"Crazy Phillip, check!" he said enthusiastically.

"One more thing I've been thinking about lately, Philip." George questioned. "Since I know you're not crazy anymore, or at least I'm reasonably sure, I need to ask you a question. You've known J.D. for a long time, and I've been wondering ... I don't really know how to ask this ... Is he a ... "

"A mobster?" Phillip asked. "Is that the right question?"

"Yeah, I guess that's what I want to know"

"Well, I wouldn't describe him as a mobster. A bootlegger, depending on your definition. He is not into prostitution, and he hasn't ever intentionally hurt anyone. He is mainly a businessman who ... gets in a hurry and occasionally takes shortcuts like the rest of us. He made a couple of mistakes early in life that he is still trying to make up for. The two of you probably know him better than anyone. He loves coming up here!"

"We love him," Alesa said. "I know people, and I don't think he's a desperado. He is like a father to me and I think I would defend him in court."

"I love him, too, and I just came from a world where everything was categorized," George said apologetically. "Forget I mentioned it!"

"Okay!" Phillip said, putting his crazy voice on as he walked out the door.

The couple went back to work and didn't sit down until later that afternoon when they were resting out on the porch. George thought about his conversation with Phillip, and he felt guilty for accusing J.D. of anything, for the *shortcuts* they felt forced to take. Like J.D., they regretted some decisions they had made, but for the most part, they made people happy and served the community as best they could.

He also felt bad because J.D. had contributed something to him in their "session" that no one else in his life ever had. He was able to share this with Alesa, and now she was better for it. This was a gift he could never repay except to share it maybe someday with others.

He had worked through most of his remorse, especially since he realized Alesa, and Phillip must have already discussed this and dismissed it. He was a little jealous, but mostly he was content. He was smoking a cigar on the porch with Ricky when the weirdest thing happened.

THE FIGHT

"WE ARE HOLDING OUT SURPRISINGLY WELL OVER HERE. I know it's difficult for those around us, especially the farmers and the bankers. Those folks have a co-dependent relationship. No offense to your father. He's making it okay, and he's not in debt, right?"

"Yeah," George responded, "he's in fair shape. But he just barely got his crops in this year, and he may finally be ready to retire. I hope so. I think I could buy him out and move him to town. On the other hand, that may open up a whole new can of worms."

"Speaking of worms, who is that guy?"

They both noticed him. Someone standing on the corner of the front of the bank staring at the hotel. He was trying to look like he was waiting for someone, but he kept looking at the cars, squinting to see a little better.

"That's O'Malley! That bastard! He's always trying to overcharge me for lumber. He just has a personal beef for some reason. I've seen him hanging out with the busybodies."

"Oh, so that's who that was with the women when they were writing down license plates. And that group from Nebraska is here now, so ... "

"He's doing it again! He's writing something down. What the hell?"

"There he is! That's O'Malley," Ricky shouted at the top of his lungs.

The shout echoed down the not-that-busy street. O'Malley stopped dead and just stared at them for nearly half a minute. He seemed like he wanted to run, but he had been called out, and they knew who he was. The baseball cap wasn't fooling anyone. He paced a little before speaking.

"Hey, you Dutch bastard, I'm going to do whatever I can to stop you. You are a bootlegger, and everyone knows it. I'm going to get you," he said, holding the pieces of paper with the license plate numbers.

"Where are your hens?" Ricky mocked.

"I know what you're doing over there, and I'm going to stop you."

George saw Phillip step out from around the corner about a block away. He was approaching slowly, probably thinking he could scare O'Malley away. He was walking slowly and looking at the two of them as if to say, *Do you need my help?*

"I'm going to put a stop to this," George said, already in motion and headed across the street.

"Don't come over here, Dutchman—I'm warning you."

"Warn me?" George yelled, now in full stride and half-way across the street.

He caught a glimpse of the bank ladies peering out the window. It was likely that everyone in town knew what was going on or what was about to happen, but no one wanted to be directly involved. Most disputes in small towns either get resolved quickly or they drag on for years. George didn't have time for this dispute, and he wanted it to end quickly. He intended for them to talk face-to-face.

"Listen, we need to talk," George started, circling the petrified O'Malley.

"Stay away from me, you Dutch, bootlegging bastard!"

"I just want to talk. We can work out the lumber bill. Why are you out to get me?"

"Because I know what's going on over there, and I'm going to do everything I can to stop you, you … bootlegger!"

"What makes you the judge? What are you doing with the money you extort from all the fine citizens? I could make a lot of assumptions about you and the pastor's wife, huh?"

"Just get away from me," O'Malley quivered as he backed away.

Everyone had a different vantage point, but no one remembered George actually punching O'Malley, just that he fell backward and cracked his head on the cement bench out front. As George reached down to help him up, O'Malley scrambled down the side street and that is when Ricky and the then-arriving Phillip noticed the sheriff sitting on the hood of his car. Calmly, the sheriff walked forward as O'Malley scrambled to safety.

"Listen, George," the sheriff said in his official voice. "I saw what happened, and I'll be over in a few minutes. Let me check on O'Malley, and I'll be over to deal with you soon."

"Wait, am I in trouble?"

The sheriff just nodded and then slowly walked back towards his vehicle. They were not that far removed from the days on the plain and the Wild West. Some days it felt like they had made progress, and other days they were so far behind the times.

"I didn't touch the bastard," George called out as he walked back to the now full porch.

Back in the shadows of the door, he saw J.D.

I didn't even know he was here, he muttered to himself. He felt a little more secure with all his friends around. There were plenty of witnesses, but sometimes the loudest spectators were the ones that didn't see anything.

"When did you get in?" George said, looking at J.D. and then gazing at all the people still gathered around him.

It reminded him of that wrestling match so long ago, but this wasn't a friendly test of strength. This was serious, and he just wanted it to be over. His mind raced as he thought about what it meant to love our enemies and various creeds and customs he had accumulated on his journey of life. What is the right thing to do when someone is trying to *get you* and dishonor your name? Should it be ignored? He realized these are the kind of decisions that make-or-break people. He loved his life, and he didn't want it destroyed.

The close allies at the hotel talked in the conference room for several minutes. Phillip, J.D., Ricky, and Nancy were there. It was comforting to George to have several close friends that generally didn't judge him, but wholeheartedly accepted him. He was different now, or he would have been hiding in his basement in fear of retribution. But today, he was able to accept the love from the close group of friends.

They were all smiling until the sheriff entered. He didn't look happy, and he walked cautiously. He rarely came to the hotel or restaurant, so he checked his surroundings before approaching the group. He was measuring every step so he kept up his tough-guy persona. George was taught to respect those in authority in the Army, and he had no reason not to trust the sheriff even though it was obvious there was a darker purpose for this visit.

"You don't remember me, do you, Popper?"

"No, I can't say that I do. You hardly ever come around."

"We were just young pups then. They used to call me Zork … from across the river!"

"Hey, man, how's it going?" George said, forgetting the situation they were in.

"After that day by the river, my life was ruined for many years. People just kept reminding me how I got beat by the army boy—that was MY legacy. I vowed to get you back, and here it is! We called it a tie, but everyone liked you more because you were pretty and had *served our country* and all that. They teased me for years."

"I am sorry you had to go through that, but I still haven't done anything wrong, and O'Malley is the one being crazy here."

"But you don't get to decide," Sheriff Zortleff scolded. "I'm in charge now!"

"And I'm crazy?" Phillip chimed in.

When someone says something strange, everyone in the crowd goes quiet. It's almost like everyone must process how to respond or think when something out of the ordinary is verbalized. There was little to no crime in the small town except maybe petty theft here and there since the depression started up. On most days, the law fought hard to stay away, and the better ones helped encourage the constituents of the town.

"O'Malley is pressing charges against you for assault. I'll be back in the morning to take your statement and see how we're going to proceed after we talk to the county."

"Wait, what? Assault? Are you kidding me?"

The crowd burst out into murmurs and groans. Many of them saw exactly what was happening and knew it was about jealousy and judgment more than anything criminal, but they remained calm and composed, mostly because it was a ridiculous charge.

"I'm profoundly serious, Army boy! Don't go anywhere!"

"I'll be right here. Want me to fix breakfast?"

"Today," Sheriff Zortleff continued, "is about someone else. I have bigger fish to fry!"

THE ARREST

"J.D. MORELLI, AKA JON DAVID MORELLI, I HAVE A WAR-
rant for your arrest on the charge of tax evasion," Sheriff Zortleff said
proudly.

As he walked quietly to the back of the room, gasps were heard
throughout, and his deputies appeared from the restaurant side of the
hotel. J.D. stood quietly with his head down and submitted. As he
was quickly ushered out of the hotel, he glanced up only long enough
to whisper to George.

"It's going to be okay," J.D. said to the couple, and then he was
gone.

Nancy and Ricky were quieting the staff and the hotel guests.
Phillip returned to his façade and acted especially crazy as a distraction until George and Alesa escaped into the back room, and then he
quickly followed, closing, and locking the door behind him. Phillip
took a deep breath, resetting his character, and glancing at the doors,
spoke quietly and directly.

"I need to talk to you two before anything else happens ... "

George paced the room, as Alesa held her head in her hands. They
could hear the mild panic outside the room, but they needed to find
some kind of plan. They were under attack, and they had never experienced anything quite like this. Joe continued, and they both considered the irony that *Crazy Phillip* was the only rational one in the
room.

"J.D. knew this was coming. He didn't want it to happen here,
but he wanted to tell you personally before it did. He's been over at
my place for a few hours, but he panicked a little when y'all got in a

disagreement on the street. He used the tunnel to sneak over here, but he didn't know the sheriff was anywhere around."

"So, what *is* going on?" George asserted, voice unsteady and obviously confused.

"As you know J.D. admitted that he took a few shortcuts in life. He regrets all his mistakes he made in the past and failing to pay taxes is about the only sin he hasn't atoned for. In a way, he was ready to go to jail just to have it be over. He's going to plead guilty and accept the sentences and fines. He's ready to lay it to rest, so that whenever he dies, his conscience is clear."

"What do we do now?" Alesa broke in, "Is George going to jail, too?"

"No," Phillip laughed, despite the panicked eyes staring back at him. "A dozen people saw what happened today. That idiot staged this whole thing. It's not going to amount to anything."

"What about business things?" George broke in. "J.D. has a lot invested in us … what do we do?"

"Conrad will be here in a few hours to explain, but basically J.D. divided up all his assets about 6 months ago. I was a recipient of a portion of that wealth. Essentially, I will become J.D. for all practical purposes as far as you are concerned. In a way, when his wife died, he lost all need to build wealth except for the challenge of it. Now that he will most likely be incarcerated for a while, he doesn't need it anymore."

"We just want things to go back to the way they were," Alesa said as the tears fell.

"I understand," Phillip said simply as he quietly left them alone.

By then, the chaos was settled, and the couple emerged reluctantly, but hand-in-hand.

The couple spoke to Nancy and Ricky first. They thanked them for their loyalty all these years. Then they went back to work. There was nothing left to do now but prepare for guests and try to be strong. When the busybodies walked by, a couple of the staff restrained Ricky as he hollered at them to stay away. He couldn't take it back, but he also didn't regret it.

Dinner that night was more like a church potluck than a restaurant. Truth be told, it was leftovers because the kitchen couldn't muster the energy for anything else. The fact that it was free drew a large crowd, and the owners and staff realized that the town wasn't against them. This provided some immediate relief from the stress of the moment. They finished the day, went to bed, and attempted to sleep and prepare for what was ahead.

The next morning George was charged with assault, given a court date, and released on his own recognizance. He gave his statement and tried not to say what he really thought. He returned to the hotel undisturbed and retreated into the lower levels. There he remained for the next few days. Alesa checked on him occasionally and left food for him where he could find it.

The hotel was quiet for the next month. Guests never knew anything was wrong, and the town went on with business as usual. The staff maintained an uncharacteristically somber mood. They assumed it wouldn't get any better when George went to trial. Part of them wanted to teach O'Malley a lesson, but they knew that's exactly what he wanted.

In the meantime, George's parents sold the farm and moved into George and Alesa's old house. They were close to town, but they still never came in unless it was necessary for supplies and such. They had a large garden and a few cattle, so they rarely needed anything.

A few days later, George emerged from the basement, showered, and went back to work just like it was a new day. When his parents walked into the restaurant, he almost passed out. He wondered if they knew, but he really didn't even care. He was numb, and he greeted them just like any other customer and seated them in the best booth he could find, nodded at Ricky, and left the room.

GEORGE AND JOE

"WHY WAS IT SO HARD TO FIND A JOB WHEN YOU'RE 55?"
Joe thought as he searched the internet for jobs. He felt like he could
do anything, but people stereotyped him. He was either considered
over-qualified, wouldn't be interested, or just simply one of too many.
He wanted to imagine there was a conspiracy, but that kind of energy
never accomplished much except to discourage him. So, he decided to
stay positive since they still had some money in the bank, and Mary
wasn't panicking.

It had been about a month since the meeting with George and
he still thought about it every day. He couldn't believe the effortless
process they went through had impacted him in such a subtle, yet
positive way.

"You don't react like you used to," Mary said abruptly one day.

"What do you mean?"

"I guess, I just don't have to walk on eggshells as much."

"I hope not," Joe said sheepishly.

"Well, I used to. It was like you stored things up and then exploded
for no reason."

"Well, it probably wasn't for *no* reason," Joe said, almost reacting
then calming down.

"You still respond to things. You should. But it's not a reaction ...
it's a response."

"And that's better?"

"Yes, definitely better," Mary nodded her head without judgment.

Joe got side-tracked from the hotel research after what happened
with George. He consulted with a counselor friend and told him
about the makeshift session he had.

"Sounds like a focusing session," Mark said.

"Oh yeah, do you use it in counseling?"

"It's not my specialty, but lots of spiritual directors use it to access the felt-sense we have of past trauma. When things happen to us that we are not equipped to deal with, we form stuck places within us that have to be accessed to help free us up. If we don't, triggers cause us to revisit those places in us, and we respond to current situations with the same coping mechanisms we used earlier in life. It's usually not effective. But, when we go there with compassion, often the trauma can be shifted, and we go forward in a different way."

"Like not reacting to situations?" Joe offered.

"Exactly," Mark said. "That's the most common thing that changes with focusing."

Since the current job opportunity didn't work out, Joe had some free time. He tried doing some writing and was able to do so freely. He always enjoyed this type of writing, where he just wrote without editing or thinking about it too much. He wondered if people would understand what he was thinking: but the intention was more how he felt than what he thought. This development of expression was occurring more often. It came naturally, but at the same time, it was unfamiliar and not part of his practice.

While Mary was at work, he returned to the center of his research. He scanned through the digital catalog for Eugene Gendlin, the founder of Focusing. Joe didn't need to go back to the shelves, but he loved the musty smell of books. He could also say he was doing something productive by getting out of the house. In the back of his mind, he was hoping he would have an epiphany and find a name or reference to look up that would help him with the hotel.

He nodded at Sara, who had started another page-turner, and headed back to his new place to scavenge. There again sat George.

George looked like many men in this town. He was overweight, later middle-aged with pants that were a little too big, and a basic, wrinkled, button-up shirt. His graying hair was thinning and disheveled as though it were a burden to even tame. He wore dated wire-rim frames with dulled, scratched lenses. Cheap sneakers or boots usually donned his feet. Signs of age and sun damage made the acne scars on his face stand out more, telling another part of his story.

Despite all this, Joe only paid attention to his eyes. They have a depth as though he listened with them. It was hard to describe, but when Joe was talking, he knew George understood him, and was looking into him. As Joe walked into the room, he saw those eyes—not eyes of judgment nor impatience. They were eyes of compassion and grace. The eyes locked on Joe's and followed him down to the table.

"How are you, friend?" George said kindly.

"Still trying to find a job, but better since we talked," Joe responded.

"How so?" George chuckled gleefully as Joe settled in.

"Mary was just telling me that I don't react to things as much as I used to. It's not that I'm ignoring issues that come up, but it's much more of a thoughtful response than an inappropriate reaction."

"How do you feel about that?"

"It's like I'm walking on new legs because I was the other way for a long time. But it's so empowering to know that it's a part of me that wants to react, and I can be in charge, and I can minister and care for myself. It's an amazing feeling to be more in control and at the same time feel freer than I have ever been."

"That's great, what's next?"

"Well, I kind of have three objectives," Joe articulated. "The first is to find a job. It's not urgent yet, but I'd love to find how I'm going to put the food on the table for the upcoming years. Second, I want to keep doing this internal searching that has brought so much awareness recently. I want to keep *focusing*, but I don't think I could do it every day—it's exhausting. Third, I want to discover more about the hotel, even though it's not that urgent."

"I have a challenge for you. Tell me about how you found the best three things in your life."

I guess the most important thing that I found in my life was when I met Mary. I was working the shift and went to the ATM. There were some girls there that invited me to a club down in the party district in the city I lived in at the time. They told me to ride with them which may or may not have been a wise idea. They were already drinking, I was always interested in being around women at that stage of my life, so I took the risk."

"So, Mary was one of the girls?"

"No, don't get ahead of yourself. We went to a popular club, and the girls darted off to a different part of the room. I later saw them dancing on tables, and I was wondering how I was going to get home when Mary walked up behind me and asked me to dance. For some reason, I knew she could be the one from the very moment I danced with her that night."

"So, how did you get home?"

"Mary and her friend drove me back to my vehicle. It was all so unlikely and random and unusual for all of us. I didn't necessarily go to those types of clubs very often; Mary wouldn't have risked driving a stranger; and it definitely wasn't something that was well planned and orchestrated.

"I found my publisher in the same way," Joe continued, "I knew it would be challenging to find a publisher, especially since I was moving away from my denomination of origin. My beliefs were changing, and I even wondered if anyone believed like me. One day, while talking to another author, I asked if he had any suggestions. He told me to try his, a boutique publisher that was interested in books by other authors just like me. It felt like a gift."

"Hmm."

"My last job was the same way. It just came to me. A guy that didn't even know me heard I was looking and suggested I try the job that led to 15 years of successful employment. He was also one of the reasons I eventually left, but again, it seemed to just kind of happen. I have this wonderful friend who has already, through her own journey, experienced spirituality directly. When I was talking about the possible success of my next book, she told me, 'Just let it happen. The work's already been done; it's already in motion!'"

"So, your three biggest successes have been when you let it come to you!"

"That's a subtle way to describe it!"

"It's what you and your mystic friend implied. When you have done the necessary prep work, sometimes you must stop *making it happen* and start *letting it happen,* do you agree?"

"I'm starting to see that," Joe said.

"Perhaps you could apply that to the hotel exploration. Instead of trying to make it happen, why don't you let it happen! You've done some prep work. You've put yourself in the right vicinity. Why don't you let *it* find *you?*"

Joe took a mental step back. He thought about other things this applied to. He always said poetry found him, not the other way around. He also knew songwriters talked about songwriting in this way. The best wisdom to raise his kids was when he was frustrated enough to listen and find new, creative answers instead of forcing his worn-out assumptions. Most times, the best, most creative solutions at work came when he was in the shower and almost gave up—and then *it* came to *him!*

George waited patiently until he could tell Joe was finished thinking.

"So, let it come to you! What if you just went to the hotel and let it happen—listen, observe, feel, sense what was there. Let the answers be revealed. There is energy and spirit all around you that wants to communicate with you just like your body did when we *focused.*"

"When the student is ready … " Joe began.

"Then the answer," George interrupted, "not necessarily a teacher, comes."

"I'm starting to put those pieces together. I'm ready! I'm ready to listen!"

George just nodded his head. He didn't give Joe the answers, but like a good companion, he listened and helped him be intuitive. He discovered kicking in doors incurred some accomplishment, but the best things came when he was ready and open, not when he manipulated situations.

It was too late for job searching, and not the right time for focusing, so he decided to go to the hotel and just listen. It sounded silly if he said it out loud, but it still was the right approach. The *why* was hard to determine or predict, but he was returning to that magic of that night when he met Mary. He wasn't expecting anything to happen, but he was open to whatever did, even if it seemed like a disappointment because he also knew those could be camouflaged detours that lead to the best destinations.

He hoped the door would be unlocked, but he could settle for a stop on the porch. Luckily, when he arrived, the door was open, ready to receive him, and enough light showed through the front windows to allow access to the front room. He sat in the chair where he had visited with Marla days earlier. He took a deep breath and went through a body scan to assess his current situation. He was having trouble at first with too many thoughts, but then, suddenly, something claimed him, and he felt a cool breeze as he relaxed.

SITTING IN THE HOTEL

SINCE LEAVING HIS CHURCH, JOE HAD BEEN DOING SOME considerably deep thinking. Much of that centered on creation. One morning, he spent several hours wondering how nature has its own drumbeat and rhythm. The animals and insects all danced in an ordered schedule and flowed together without any obvious guidance or instruction. There was built-in intelligence to the way they weaved nests and gathered and stored food. Some might call it instinct, but Joe understood it to be inherent intelligence.

He almost stopped this train of thought because of his upbringing. The church and his culture had taught him to stick only to that which he knew and not to dream beyond safe boundaries. After all, he was supposed to be investigating the hotel, and here he was thinking about nature and animals and such. Then, he heard the words of George.

"Just let it happen!"

So, he let his mind go and opened to whatever might come to him. Whenever he contemplated nature, he slipped right into the quizzical structure of plants. Recently, Joe had begun cultivating broccoli, alfalfa, and radish sprouts. These little greens contained so much nutrition which then spurred his curiosity about all those phytonutrients contained within one tiny seed. And what about the inherent intelligence to create each new plant? Every. Single. Seed.

These kinds of thoughts led him to imaginations about God. He understood why some people refer to God as *source* when he considered the seeds and the plants. He understood how God could be *in* all things when he observed the intelligence inherent in a robin constructing a nest or an acorn sprouting into a giant tree. He released his mind and himself from his need for certainty and explanation and just wondered about it all.

Nature always seemed relaxing even when he thought about its complexity. But eventually his mind always returned to humans. As he sat in the quiet hotel, a part of himself was transported back in time. He could almost hear the bustle of the adjacent restaurant. He heard the clanking, slurping, and chatter that comes along with serving breakfast in a small space. He imagined that scene from every movie where the experienced waitress skillfully manages the dance of activity much like the animals and plants survive in their own environments.

Joe imagined a scene where the waitress catches his eye. He sees the experience, the weariness, and the pain all wrapped up in one glance. She shoots a look, like *I can't handle one more* and then she returns to her duties. Her smile is genuine, but just enough to make people feel comfortable. She also carries this inherited intelligence and when she is tuned in, she can also serve as therapist, nurse, and life coach—all instinct, no official training.

An audible disagreement at the front desk. The clerk is younger, in her 30s, breathtakingly beautiful and understated. She is obviously in charge because she speaks with authority to the customer yet manages to win him over. Her inherited wisdom comes from somewhere inside. It's experience, but this is a person who has tapped into something deeper inside herself that makes her strong and ambitious, despite the pain that gnaws at her from time to time.

Joe almost criticized himself out of the imagination. That old critical part of himself wanted to call off this useless exercise of his feelings and inclinations. *We could be doing some real looking*, it whispered to him. But he dismissed the critic for now and took a deep breath. He wasn't thinking so much about the hotel. He was feeling it.

A rush of emotions flooded through his body as images of guests floated through his mind like whispers and ghosts from the past. He saw small families and businessmen and shifty characters. He felt their laughter and anxiety and their determination to stick to the itinerary and the thousands of disagreements and embarrassments. There was the occasional meltdown by young and old and every so often, the romantic passion of two people in love!

Through all the whispers and emotions and activity of the hotel, Joe regularly caught glimpses of the main characters. There was the chef that every so often emerged from the kitchen. Not just a fry cook, he choreographed the dance in the restaurant. In much the same way, another employee emerged as the conductor of all things business at the front desk. But the consistent heartbeat of the establishment obviously flowed through the couple that often just observed together as they whispered to each other and beckoned to others that served the hotel.

Joe wondered whether all this was just a mosaic of past movie clips that he was piecing together, but something about it felt deeper than just a memory. This was something being shared with him as much as he was discovering it. For whatever reason, his desire to participate in the history of the hotel brought the soul of the place to him. Then suddenly, the dance changed, and all the ancillary characters left the stage.

The couple stood in the corner and looked towards Joe with welcoming eyes. He wanted to call them *eyes of grace*, but it made him think about church, so he just identified them as *eyes of compassion*. Their eyes drew him in and for a few seconds he could feel what they were feeling.

He felt their love for the hotel, almost like they were beckoning him to observe and appreciate what they loved so much. He also understood their attention and care for people. There was an external focus that held their attention long enough to express that other people were of utmost concern. But beneath their love and compassion and joy was a deep pain that felt oddly relatable to Joe. That is where he landed for the next few minutes.

As he began to cry, his inner voice tried to tell him to *grow up and stop being a baby*, but he dismissed it momentarily and just let himself empathically channel the young couple. He wanted to hug them, realized it was impossible, so he found a new level deep inside him and melted into what he was feeling. There was a deep knowing that this was the right thing to do. He wanted to ease their pain and make them feel something different. Yet in that moment, the right thing to do was just to feel this together.

"Are you okay?" the voice whispered.

"Yeah," he said softly, not making the connection at first.

He almost fell off his chair when he realized Marla was in the room. His mind raced, but when he realized there was no immediate danger, he returned his head to his hands and tried to compose himself. After a few deep breaths, he sat upright and began to speak while he stared at the corner where he *saw* the couple. A part of him wanted them to come back and another part wished they wouldn't have shared this burden with him.

"I … Uh … I think I just met the hotel owners," Joe said.

"What do you mean? The Poppers?"

"Yes, they were right there. I could see … Well, I felt … No, I don't know what it was, but I feel like I know them now, and I have a thousand questions. I think I need to go home and get some rest."

Marla didn't say much. She just seemed to understand. She was one of the few people that would understand. She patted him on the shoulder, and he shuffled to the front door.

"What just happened?" He turned to ask.

"You're going to need some time to digest this," she said.

A thousand thoughts raced through his mind as he drove back to his house. A new challenge arrived at his phone as it rebooted. Another rejection email for his employment search. Instead of obsessing though, he tossed it on the couch and curled up in his recliner. His past taught him to distrust anything unusual even though it was supposed to be a life of faith and wonder. Everything was wrapped up in certainty and this experience wasn't confined to any box that he knew much about.

Joe wondered why he feared direct experience. He knew he longed for the adventure of the unknown, but in the back of his mind, he often managed those excursions to the point of simply being cause and effect studies manifested in actionable intelligence. He knew that adventure and excessive planning were mutually exclusive, but he often couldn't resist, thereby, ruining the experience for everyone.

But, for some reason (possibly because of George's advice), he just *let it happen* and what was supposed to occur did. Because this was a rare occasion, he immediately began to connect the other experiences in his life that happened when he did NOT try to orchestrate them and simply let the embodied wisdom of all parts of the adventure be what they were supposed to be. He thought about his sprouts in the window. When he simply kept them wet for a few days, they did everything they were supposed to do. The same was true in the hotel.

This kind of occurrence is traumatic for a heavy thinker. He realized how much time he had spent throughout his life planning, organizing, and projecting what his life would be like and how it would manifest itself. He wondered how much more he could have achieved with a better understanding of how to tap into the wisdom that was there and let it be. It left him with even more questions.

How much of my life have I short-circuited by my fear and control?

What might my relationship have been if I just experienced them for what they were?

How have I misinterpreted the Divine because of my need to prove my point?

What is my next move … Wait … That's the wrong question … Ugh.

The urge to sleep was beginning to overtake him. His mind wasn't at all clear, and new discoveries exhausted him. For a second, he accepted that today's experience was a true adventure, not achieved by research and planning and control of every obstacle. It was the adventure that was supposed to happen, and he simply stepped into the flow. He kept the seeds wet and they sprouted. No need to spiritualize or contextualize with religious jargon to spin it into something else. It was an adventure. It was an experience. It was real, and he was grateful!

MARY

"How's the search going?" Mary said from across the living room.

Joe and Mary spent most evenings like this. Mary was most often busy with preparing for work, working on doing something for the kids (who are all grown), or texting or messaging her vast array of friends. Joe was also occupied blogging or researching his next project. They never dreamed about vacations and other places - this was the dream, and they were living it out.

Occasionally, one of them would realize they were in their own little world and say something to the other. This was most often problematic because the other was engrossed in whatever they were doing, and the speaker always had to repeat. They would lightly scold and correct each other, but most often it didn't cause an argument because whichever one interrupted the silence could very easily see themselves on the other side of the argument.

When Joe didn't answer, that was Mary's chance to get in a little dig. Since, in this instance, she was being ignored and she could give an accusation that implied he never listened or something along those lines. It was all part of the dance and usually for fun and not malicious.

"Are you listening?" Mary said, raising her voice a little.

"Actually, I wasn't, sorry."

"I was asking about your investigation into the hotel. Have you found out anything new?"

"Not too much. I mean, I haven't found the kind of things I thought I would find, but I've been uncovering some other things."

"Such as?" Mary probed.

Joe felt so inadequate at this. He could write a thousand words on the subject of faith or spirituality or whatever emotionally charged him; but when it came to these kinds of nuanced topics that were difficult to explain, he usually just liked to sort through them in his mind until he could articulate them clearly. Probably some past trauma from those horrific middle school years or something.

"Let me start with the latest. I hope you don't think I'm weird," he said apologetically.

"Of course, I won't think you're weird, I already know you are. That's why I married you."

"All right, so. . . I just decided to go down to the hotel after what George said."

"Wait, who is George?"

Sometimes he called her *Captain Obvious* because she preferred not to operate in vagueness. If a story lacked detail, Mary couldn't just gloss over it or ignore it. She had to fill in *all* the blanks before proceeding. But it was an obvious omission, just like most of the other details of the story. Joe wanted to condense and just share the important parts although Mary understood very often the things that do not appear significant turn out to be the most important.

"Oh yeah. George is this dude that appeared out of nowhere at the library. He is always there when I am, and he said he could help me with investigating the hotel. But so far, he has only helped *me* with myself. I'm not complaining because, as you mentioned, I have been less reactive towards you. He is the one who helped me *focus* on the part of me that was kind of stuck. It definitely made a difference."

"Where is he from? Does he work around here?"

Joe kind of froze for a second. He didn't know anything about George. He wasn't even sure that he lived in town. Joe just always found him at the library. He knew Mary was about to ask him to fill in the blanks for everything he didn't know about George. To avoid that inevitable conversation, he interrupted.

"I don't know anything else about him, but something about him made me trust him."

She responded with the *look*, but he acted like he didn't see her eyes staring at him over her black frames.

"Anyway, the last time I saw George, he told me to 'let it happen.'"

"Let *what* happen? What does that mean?"

"I don't know what it means, but I think it means I should stop controlling?"

"Stop controlling what?" she continued with the inquisition.

"Well, it's like when we go on vacation. . . "

"Okay, okay," she said with a hand raised for him to stop before she had to relive that painful story.

Joe had a long history with over planning adventures. Planning and control helped him in the business world, but it wasn't highly effective for things like family vacations. A rigid itinerary and dogged determination to stay on schedule had caused consternation and usually led to lengthy arguments and hurt feelings. It was similar to what happened in the beginning of this original investigation of the hotel: He imagined how it would go, and when it didn't go exactly that way, he absorbed the disappointment, processed it as rejection and started reacting to that pain. In most cases, this pain was self-induced and had little to do with the current events.

"So. . . " Joe said, trying to regain the platform. "He suggested that I don't try to organize and control the investigation, but just let it come to me."

Mary was pleased with the change of direction and nodded approvingly but exercised enough wisdom not to clap or dance. She was always sensitive to his feelings and didn't pile on excessively even when she might have wanted to.

"Okay, just let me tell you what I think of this, then you can ask questions," he offered.

"Go ahead"

"I went to the hotel and just sat in the chair ... in the lobby ... to sit for a while. When my mind cleared, I noticed that I was thinking about the seed. You know, the thought process I have been going through about how all the intelligence for the plant is in the seed. I don't know why that came to mind. There was nothing there that had to do with my sprouts in the garden. I was just contemplating the simple act of watering them eventually led to the inevitable growth without any force on my part. It's the same way with the hotel—it will reveal itself to me or something like that. Maybe that's why I was thinking about that?"

"Does it matter at this point?" Mary suggested ignoring the side glance he shot her.

"Probably not," he dismissed. "Anyway ... So then, I started just *seeing visions* of people in the hotel. Sometimes there was a kind of pause and I saw them busy at work or a river of families and businessmen hustling and bustling with suitcases and bags. But, before Marla found me, there was this scene where I saw the hotel owners, where I could see their faces. It may sound odd, but it was like I could *feel* what they were feeling."

"That doesn't sound odd," she offered, leaning into his confession. "I mean it's interesting, but how did it make you feel?"

"I'm not sure how I felt, but I know they radiated *compassion*. They had a deep love for the hotel, like it was an extension of them, and they wanted me to appreciate it, too. But I also saw how their lives and the hotel brought trauma to their existence. They seemed to be ... I don't know ... asking for help sorting through this mysterious part of the human experience."

"I think we all can relate to that?" she said.

"It's funny," he continued. "When this adventure began, I wanted to put the owners in a convenient, definable *box*. Basically, stereotype them. It's what those I interviewed also wanted. They would say things like 'He was a good guy' or 'He did good things for the community,' as though they needed to reach a verdict so that the explanation was easier to manage. But having that vision just reinforced the notion that people are remarkably complex, and the struggles of life are somewhat consistent for everyone despite the time differences. There is some inherent pain in the human experience and although the times were different, we all have similar struggles."

"That's so true, so where do you go from here?"

"That's just it, I think I'm okay with just letting it happen. I still have some questions. But I'm starting to get that this investigation is about more than I thought it would be. What we all want is to discover what is in the caverns and recesses of our lives. I really have less certainty about this than when I began, but I'm okay with that."

"I should visit with George. I'm not as perfect as you think I am. Perhaps, he could help me get on track."

In Joe's mind, Mary was about as perfect as he could hope for. But there were things in her past that were still rooted inside her. Just like he reacted to things when triggered, she occasionally struggled with things that never got resolved. Like most people, there were parts of her that were *stuck*.

"I think you should," Joe offered. "I wonder why nobody ever taught us about how to deal effectively with trauma. I feel like most of our religious experiences were more about bypassing our wounds than treating them. I wish that were not true, but it is."

"It's most definitely true!"

"So, even the hotel owners walk around with this woundedness, and we often can't find a solution. Religion gives us some clues, but it mostly leaves us hoping for something miraculous to magically take it away. Knowledge helps us some because we can rationalize what makes us *tick* and we can develop better strategies. But some of these strategies and practices are also a form of bypassing. I don't think the key to getting better is any of these things."

"Then what is it? What's the answer?"

"I don't know, but I think that may be what this quest is about."

After 30 years of marriage, they sometimes communicated even in silence. It was obvious that both were pondering the moment. They were opposites in so many ways, but both of them had a deep longing to help people get better. It was expressed so differently in each of them, but the root desire was the same. They longed for kindness, mercy, empathy, and love in the world, and when it didn't happen, they became disheartened and exasperated. At times, they lost hope, but at times like this they allowed themselves to dream a little.

MORE SECRETS

FOR SOME TIME, JOE HAD ENJOYED WALKING, NOT JUST AS a means of exercise but as a release. When too many thoughts filled in his mind, he would find clarity and the ability to sort through the options in his life on a simple stroll. He made most decisions on the walking trail or in the shower.

Since Mary was working, and he didn't have much to do, he decided to walk the normal path that they visited daily. He was thinking of the hotel, and it caused his mind to drift to the past, especially when he saw an older building or something that seemed slightly out of place.

As he rounded a corner, he noticed the creek that ran through town. He imagined that downstream there might once have been a still dripping moonshine. He knew that many homes in this neighborhood were built in the 1920s, so he could see through their architecture a connection to the past. The downtown buildings were the same way. Some had more modern renovations but some of them held to the past like the guy that wears retro clothes even when they aren't retro.

His usual course was about a mile, and they would walk about two laps together. This time alone on the first lap, he noticed a text from his son-in-law Travis. Earlier in the day, he had asked him about the tunnels in town because he remembered him mentioning it once before. His text indicated that the entrance was behind the community building. Oddly enough, it was about this time that his walk was a couple hundred yards away nearing the back side of that building. He could see a garage door size opening on the back of the theater/ gathering place.

"Hmm," was all he could say.

One thing you don't do in a small town is stare too long. Everyone always knows what everyone is doing, but it's rude to let people know that you are the one reporting the news. It can also be dangerous to poke your nose in someone else's business, thus part of the reason for the phrase, *Let sleeping dogs lie.* However, it is appropriate for people to stare when people walk into the café because *locals are simply trying to figure out who they are.*

Joe pondered the reason for having that many tunnels. Was it just like novelty or was there a reason to have that many underground boroughs? If they were that extensive, there would have to be almost town-wide involvement. It just kind of spun around in his head as he continued walking. He was coming to the spot where Gaston insisted on leaving a deposit and he battled with being embarrassed and finding humor and glee in the entire process of trying to keep a dog from taking a dump. He was glad he decided to leave him at home so he could think more clearly.

He didn't even debate taking the second lap. He was in full stride when Charlie appeared at the front of his business. He called out to Joe, waving him over to meet on Main Street. Joe was slightly uncomfortable after their previous and past encounters.

"Hey, I got something I want to show you," Charlie said reluctantly, looking around.

"Okay, what's up?"

"Follow me," Charlie said, leading him around the side of the building next to his business.

Joe had seen the business several times from a distance. It appeared a bit older or less maintained than the rest of the street. The writing on the front window was faded, so he could barely make out any of the words, but he thought one of the words was *auto.* Charlie walked the length of the building on the side street back to the small door that was the primary entrance. The dirty glass windows revealed up close an older style filling station just like you would see in the classic movies. As they entered, there were old oil cans and other preserved memorabilia despite the random accumulated layers of junk.

To the right, Charlie led him into the establishment past an average-looking repair garage, soils and stains emitting fumes of toxicity, to which he just kind of waved his hand and stopped to let Joe take it all in. It was obviously the infamous car dealership and repair facility once co-owned by the late Mr. Popper.

"This was once a dealership and garage," Charlie shared. "I felt bad after our conversation the other day. Part of me didn't want to talk about it because I was afraid you would think worse of the town, but I also didn't want to lie to you. I want to set the record straight. I know we've had our differences, but overall, I think it's best if we shoot straight with each other—I certainly don't like lying."

"I appreciate that," Joe offered.

"But this is not what I wanted to show you, there's more."

"Lead on."

Charlie continued through the dank space to a door blocked by layers of trash and boxes thick with dirt and dust. The door loudly creaked open stirring dust that fluttered down around him, but he continued with confidence like he had been there recently.

"We discovered this room several years ago after we bought the place."

There wasn't much in the smaller room except a large counter and another door beyond that. A worn curtain hung over the door, as a border but struggled to stay secured. There were no wall hangings and only a couple of boxes—just a plain old room with another door.

"So," Charlie said, "that door leads to the tunnels. Well, it did anyway. It's boarded up down there, and the stairs are a bit treacherous, but the previous owner showed me and explained that this might have once been a place to buy liquor and gain access to the speakeasy across the street."

"Really?"

"Yeah," Charlie continued, "well, you know, the heyday of the hotel was back during Prohibition. It wasn't so much that the town was against it as much as the authorities. So, this town, along with Mr. Popper, must have had some kind of big operation. I think they wanted to keep the focus off the front of the hotel 'cause a lot of the temperance folks were always watching that side of things. You know how it is; anyone from out of town is suspect."

"Right, like me?"

"You are a newcomer, so yeah!"

"I've been here for 10 years, Charlie!"

"That's like a stranger in a small town," Charlie chuckled.

"Yeah, I stopped fighting it a long time ago."

"But, hey, the door and the tunnel are not the most interesting thing I want to show you. It's this!"

He reached down below the counter to reveal what he had hidden there for some time, wrapped in cloth, and covered in dust and cobwebs. Apparently, he hadn't shown it to anyone in a few years.

"It's a shovel," Charlie said.

"I can see that. Is that significant or is there more to the story."

The shovel was small like he pictured a soldier carrying to dig latrines, but it's handle had been broken and the spoon part was either partly rusted off or had also been broken a little. But, even at that, there didn't seem to be an obvious story, until Charlie elaborated.

"There *is* more to the story. We found the shovel in that wall," as he pointed to a picture leaning up against the lower portion of the wall behind the counter. "One day we discovered this hole behind the picture because mice were leaving droppings around this area. It was plastered shut but sloppily painted and not sealed very well. It made us wonder why it was there at all."

"Hmmm ... Yeah ... I see what you mean."

"Yeah, everyone has a shovel. But, why hide it in the wall? There has to be a lot more to the story and I'd love to know the answer. Probably never will, but it's interesting."

"This is exactly why I started on this quest; it is fascinating."

"That's all I have. I just wanted to come clean about what I know. I wish I had a million dollars, and I would help you excavate the tunnels. We could make it a tourist trap," Charlie laughed, then stopped himself from enjoying the idea too much and shook his head to indicate he needed to come back to reality.

"Count me in," Joe said, "if you ever make that happen."

"And maybe you could come see us at church some time."

Joe knew that Charlie had been waiting to slip that in, but he didn't take offense.

"Probably not going to happen, but maybe I can help you clean up the building and look around for some more treasures. I really appreciate this."

"No problem, brother," he said, feeling his evangelical roots.

Since the side road was his route to finish the walk, Joe started that way, and they nodded awkwardly to each other before leaving. He finished his walk feeling refreshed and new.

He hoped some day they would create time travel. He didn't want to go back and change things—he just wanted to ask questions. He wanted to ask Martin Luther King, Jr., what it felt like to stand for something that took his life. He wanted to ask the first astronaut what it was like to walk on the moon. And to the owner of the car dealership, he wanted to know why he hid a shovel in his wall.

He thought about Charlie as he fell asleep and wondered whether they would be friends. Probably not. Neither one of them was outgoing enough to put the effort into making it work, but they could definitely be more cordial now that they shared a secret. Joe wondered whether that might be part of being an insider in a small town. Maybe it's not just that people shared experiences—it might also be that they shared secrets!

Joe was edging on deep slumber, when he sat straight up in bed, remembering two random but key facts. When Marla was droning on about the hotel, she mentioned them. The first was a hole in the ceiling where they found a plate of chicken bones (something he still wanted to investigate) and something they found in a wall of one of the rooms—a shovel. Wait, maybe he read that in one of the articles. He searched frantically through his phone for a picture and there it was!

One shovel in the wall makes it interesting! Two shovels, inside two different walls, is bizarre!

"Oh well," he thought. "So much for taking a nap."

1938 — GEORGE'S DAD

As George sat at the table in the conference room eating breakfast, he couldn't help but take inventory of his life. Although there was talk of global unrest and a possible war, those kinds of things seemed so far away from his perfect environment. The country was still experiencing repercussions from the Great Depression, but because of their frugality and wisdom, they were not only surviving, but they also thrived. Everything was working well for them.

George had taken J.D.'s advice and snatched up some farmland when it was dirt cheap and now was beginning to slowly rent it out. In some cases, it was the same farmland the tenants used to own that they now rented from the hotel owner. The hotel was almost always booked solid, and the people enjoyed, not only the hotel but all the other endeavors the couple had masterminded including the speakeasy that existed apart from the eyes of the busybodies.

He nodded to Alesa, and she knew what he meant. He was going out to take a morning walk. It was usually on Friday when he finally had time to walk the downtown area and survey not only what they had accomplished, but what was possible for the near future. People greeted him warmly, but his mind was a little deeper in thought and something was drawing him away from his normal path. Usually, he at least stopped into the businesses they owned, but today he continued on. Something else was gnawing at him. He made it to one end of town and walked back up the street.

He passed the community building and noticed Crazy Phillip hauling a load of dirt from the back alley. He had abandoned hope of knowing the plans of his friend, so he just smiled briefly and went back to investigating his uneasiness. The town was waking up, and he didn't want to get into a conversation, so he focused forward and ignored most of what he saw until he passed the hotel and had to stop and breathe it in from this fresh perspective. He assumed this must be what parents feel like when they see their kids grow up. It was over-whelming, especially when his mind flashed back to that other time he was standing in the middle of the street.

His stomach knotted up, and he felt again the shame he felt that night. He almost stumbled another block down the street before he could catch his breath. Seeking some relief, he finally turned right on the side street only to realize he was in the exact same spot where his father lifted him into the wagon, and the nightmare began.

George sunk to the ground and crumpled up against the brick wall. The unevenness of the bricks scraping against his back only enhanced the memory of that night. He had made so much progress in dealing with his past, but the memory remained vivid and certainly something he didn't intend to encounter today. Everything in his life was blessed except one night—that one mistake—the experience he couldn't forget. He buried his head between his knees and cried uncontrollably for several minutes before he stood.

When he arose, he wasn't hurt anymore, he was angry. He started down the side road and took an immediate left and made his way out to the state highway. His head was spinning, but his muscles were on fire, and he had a sense he was walking as fast as he had ever walked. His footsteps echoed in his head because of the state of his mind and adrenaline. He sensed his breath was heavy, but he couldn't tell whether he labored or overwhelmed. He knew exactly where he was going, but not exactly why.

The three-quarter mile hike luckily avoided traffic since everyone was usually working or had lost their car to the crash. At different moments of the day, he would have to deal with people offering to help, and he wasn't close to ready to talk, except for the one person that he knew he had to confront. It was imminent—not like a show-down but more like an urgency. He felt like this might be his last chance to say what needed to be said.

He turned off the dirt road and slowed his pace so much that at some point he almost stopped as tears blurred his vision. He felt ashamed of the emotional weakness and was grateful no one could see him. At one moment, he almost pivoted in retreat, but he sensed this might be the last time he ever had the courage to make this journey.

As he made his way up the walk, he noticed the enhancements. Almost everywhere he observed, everything seemed more organized. There were artfully arranged flower beds and decorations, simple but precise, indicative of care for the old homestead. Or rather his mother knew the neighbors were watching, but he still appreciated how meticulous she was and that she was responsible.

As he walked forward, he saw her sitting in an old chair next to the garden. She had obviously been laboring to gather up some pro-duce and took a break to drink a glass of tea or lemonade. That was like her. She smiled warmly but didn't get too excited and slowly rose to embrace her son. She was loving but stoic and controlled. It was the way she was and not even his father could alter her demeanor and temperament. She measured her care and love to just what was reasonable.

"Your father is in the barn," she said as if she knew why he was there.

George wasn't in a condition to analyze now; he was feeling every-thing! His head was still spinning, and the anger he felt began to subside which slowed his pace. His emotion returned to the pit of his stomach until mostly what he felt was fear. He wasn't afraid of any man. What most overpowered him were these feelings and emotions that wouldn't leave.

"What do you want?" His father said almost immediately without looking up from turning the hay with his pitchfork.

His father was much frailer than the last time they spoke, but there was something about him that still caused George to shudder. Those hands. They seemed more powerful than anyone else he had ever known. They served him well for leading a team of horses or milking cows, or, on rare occasions, beating his son. Much more than his voice, they were the way he communicated with the world. They did work, they carried bounty, and they communicated for him.

"We need to talk," George said resolutely.

"Oh, we do, do we? You finally have time to venture out to see your family. We just assumed you were too busy taking advantage of farmers and living the fancy life in town. And then, I can't even go to the church or the lumberyard without hearing about your bootlegging and whatever else goes on at that hotel. Your mother cries a lot thinking about you children."

George expected this. The cycle of shame and guilt and blame ran deep within him. The depression and changes in society only made it worse because he was fighting an internal battle that he could never win. His pseudo religion and small group of neighbors only made it worse and helped him bypass any possibility of recovery. His problems were everyone else's fault, and his only hope was doing something with his hands every day that occupied his mind enough to forget about *his* past.

"Dad, I know you're angry at the way things turned out. I know you are disappointed in me. But I just wanted to talk to you about what happened that night we went to town and what happened afterward."

His father turned slowly, releasing the fork to rest on the pillar and took a couple of steps forward. George noticed himself trembling but couldn't stop it even though he was much stronger and more able than his elderly father. His mind flashed back to the past, and he was able to draw a breath to help him come back to the present.

"Yeah, really?" his father shouted. "You want to talk about how you forever ruined my reputation in town. To this day, most of those people in town won't speak to me."

"That's because they don't even know you—you never even come to town anyway. It's all in your mind. It was that night, and it is now! We were just boys blowing off steam. You've let it ruin your entire life, and it's not my fault! It's your choice to live like this!"

"Don't you sass me boy! I'm still your father."

"I'm not sassing you," George said choking up a little, "I'm just telling you how I feel. It's what adults do, but you can't allow for people to speak their mind because you can't control situations that way. If us or mom—"

"You leave your mother out of this, I've had about enough of her mouth too!"

"Can you hear yourself! Come on, give up! How can you love something you have to control? It hasn't ever worked. It's never going to work. Why can't you just release all that fear and guilt and bitterness? Just let it go!"

"It's just not how I am," his father said thoughtfully. "I don't intend to change. . . I am who I am."

"Even if it drives everyone away from you? Even if you're terribly unhappy? Even if you can't have real friends or real conversations?"

"All that stuff is overrated. I'm happy just being here on my farm. 'Til you steal it from me in the next panic."

George turned around and took a deep breath. He was far from over the pain his father had introduced into his life; but he was becoming more able to respond instead of reacting. He loved his father, but he couldn't continue being traumatized by him.

"Okay, dad, here it is. Please let me finish. I love you and mom very much. I may not have shown you in the way you felt I should, but at various points, I had to make decisions that were best for me. At times, I have fun and stop working. I have succeeded in business, and I won't apologize for that. I can't be exactly what you want me to be, because, in my opinion, you're wrong about how you see life. Just like I can't change you, you can't change me. You may be my father, but our roles have changed. I hope you understand."

"Yeah, I understand that I failed as a parent."

George recognized this ploy. When the argument went this way, it was a shaming statement that actually meant he failed as a son to do what was expected and now carried the blame. It's the old passive aggressive reaction that he was accustomed to. If George succumbed to this, he would very soon be reminded of all the things he should be ashamed of.

"Don't start down that road, dad! I forgive you for whatever mistakes you made, and I admit the things I did wrong. I just want you to apologize and recognize what is true so that we might have a more genuine relationship for whatever time we have left."

His father pivoted to face the hay and return to his chore, mumbling to himself. George knew the conversation was just about over, so he offered one last invitation.

"So, can you just say you're sorry and tell me you love me or in any way show me you've changed."

"You're not turning me into some town folk, weakling … Like I said, I am who I am."

George started to speak about a dozen times, took a few steps, opened his mouth, but finally he conceded. He could hear his father mumbling to himself as he opened the barn door and walked away.

"I'm sorry," his father said, still facing the ground.

But it was too late, George was already past his mother and headed at full pace down the dirt road. This time his head was clear. He knew somewhere deep inside that he had represented that part of himself that was wounded. It was almost like he and the younger version of himself were walking away from the homestead into the future. He almost laughed when he thought about mooning the lumberyard owner, but eventually his pace slowed, and he could breathe again.

The relationship with his father might never be repaired. What was different now was he couldn't control his father today, but his father ultimately could not control him any longer. The things that happened to him were unfortunate, and they needed to be acknowledged, but they didn't have to have dominion over him. What he couldn't process years ago, he now could hold and nurture and heal.

He barely even noticed the walk home except that he could only think about Alesa and embracing her like he so wanted to embrace his dad. In his mind, he understood technically why his father was that way, but he couldn't accept that people can't change—because he had. He felt free and released as he walked into the hotel. At first, he was smiling at everyone but then saw his wife and melted.

He couldn't stop the tears, and he couldn't form words as they embraced. Then she quietly pulled him back to the conference room.

"Are you okay?"

"I went out to talk to Dad. I told him everything."

"How did he respond?"

"Like normal. He is just 'who he is.' But I'm different and I got it all out! It feels so freeing! I think I can move on."

"So, what about him?" Alesa said thoughtfully without judgment.

"He is responsible for his own choices. For the first time, I put all that on him. I'm not carrying it anymore."

For a while they sat on the couch and held each other until they were interrupted by business. They slipped into the kitchen with Ricky and gobbled a quick lunch before returning to the normal pace of the day. At the end of the long day, they closed the restaurant doors, set the sign for the front desk, and headed for bed. Alesa stopped George near the bedroom door.

"Okay, I think I'm ready!"

"Ready for what, I'm too tired to … "

"No, just to talk. I want to tell you about that *big deal* that I have never been able to talk about."

She peered at him intensely. Then, he nodded with his most serious, compassionate gaze.

"I'm here for you!"

For a split second, his mind flashed back to earlier that day. He shook his head to reset his attention on Alesa who needed him more, walked over to shut the outer doors, and whispered to his wife, "Okay, tell me how you feel."

ALESA'S BIG DEAL

GEORGE AND ALESA WERE AMAZINGLY MATURE FOR THEIR age. Running the hotel had forced them into roles that required focus and ingenuity. Fortunately, they made many wise decisions and took any lessons of failure and success to heart. Consequently, they were well respected in town and by their employees. As anyone in leadership knows, being favored means it's harder to admit weakness. Leaders often say, "Of course, I struggle, but who can I tell?"

In many ways, Alesa was the true leader of all the Popper enterprises. She was strong and decisive and had a knack for what makes things work. She was always one step ahead of George, and he preferred to work behind the scenes and strategize new ways to make money. She was the one who *made all his dreams come true*. But, like other leaders, there were parts of her that were still stuck. They are what Carl Jung called "shadow." J.D. had introduced the couple to these ideas, but it took years to peel back the layers of the onion.

"Even though we grew up in different towns," she started, pointing out generally toward the street, "and things were probably much like you remember. Kids played outside and most of them worked for their parents to *build a better life*. When we finally got to play, we played with all our might even though we were already tired. We went to bed exhausted. In many ways, it was the best life. We never realized we were struggling because everyone was."

George listened intently to Alesa, who would occasionally pause, then continue.

"As you know, my parents were demanding. We bought the hotel from my uncle, and all the men in that family were the same way. They were on a mission. Anything that derailed them made them angry and they responded with harshness and shaming. My mother was a perfectionist and so she fed into the dance, making it sometimes hard to find any peace or place where I felt appreciated. Over the years, I have sorted through the positive messages from that upbringing and thrown away some of the toxic shame that came with it."

"I agree," George said. "You've come a long way!"

"It felt like overnight I began to develop as a woman. In those days, we didn't talk about it *at all*, except the constant reminders to cover up. That always confused me that something that happened naturally would be a source of shame, but it became that to some extent. Boys certainly paid more attention to me. At first, they just made fun of us girls, but later they started acting like boys do. I navigated most of that well. I kissed my first boy and, at various times, explored other things. Part of me felt energized to have this new process happening inside me. It was just as confusing as it was exciting. I cried as much as I laughed, but all of us were going through the same things, so that helped."

"I remember being uncomfortable, but also excited about it." George added awkwardly.

Alesa continued, "But the big thing—what I want to talk about—happened when I was almost 16. As you know, we went to church regularly. It wasn't a discussion even; it was just what we did. There were Sunday morning and evening services. Wednesday nights the choir practiced, and the youth and children played games and had Bible lessons. There were many things I liked about church, but it was like most things—there was never a vote; it was just what we did."

"Same for us," George said, raising his hand.

"One day, the pastor announced that we had a new youth leader. Justin was a freshman at seminary and wanted to help out on Wednesdays and with youth activities. He was the most interesting mix of youth and adult. He was popular with his almost-beard, but he was still young enough to run and play games with the little kids. He wasn't handsome, but he was a grownup that the kids loved because he was sort of one of us. Justin gave me a reason to go to church. I could relate to the way he explained things, and it made religion bearable at first."

"And then?" George questioned anxiously. He intuitively knew where this was going.

"I probably was just an oblivious almost 16-year-old girl and didn't notice the signals. He would ask me to help get ready for youth activities, but more importantly, to stay after. When he hugged me goodbye, it felt warm and natural at first, but each time it started to feel different. The last time he hugged me for a long time. As I pulled away, he kissed me. At first, I kissed him back. My hormones were raging, and a part of me wanted to continue down this road. But it didn't feel right. I didn't have those kinds of feelings for him. It would have been just responding to urges."

"You have always been mature, even back then," George offered though his protective instincts set his hair on edge. He knew this was all in the past, but this was still his wife, and he wanted to hurt anyone who ever hurt her. He swallowed these emotions begrudgingly and ducked back into listening mode.

"That was when he kind of went. . . crazy. He said, 'Don't be a tease,' and started pawing at me. He was rubbing up against me, fondling my breasts, trying to get his hand inside my skirt. I couldn't even scream because all my energy was directed toward fighting him off. He had his hand fully inside my shirt," the tears trickled, and Alesa's breathing became rapid. The full effect of the event resurfaced and unsteadied her, but she persisted. She needed to let this go. "I remember your wrestling match down by the river and how exhausted you and that other guy would be after a few minutes. That's how I felt, I couldn't scream, and I couldn't even think beyond just trying to counter his moves. All I could say was 'no', but I didn't even have the energy to even scream out."

George's eyes filled with tears for his wife. Tears of pain and sorrow but also tears of hate and despair of not being there to save her. He wanted to hold her, but he knew she wasn't ready.

"There's more, but it won't help to tell all the gory details. He never got *inside* me because eventually he was as tired as me. He took a step back and bent over to breathe, and that is when I ran out into the sanctuary trying to get my clothes back on and screaming something about God and hell and damnation. I was still trying to catch my breath, but I had enough energy to make it out of the church. I glanced back through the window and caught a glimpse of him in the office—I think he was crying."

George was wrecked by the story, but he kept quiet.

"We lived within a mile of the church. I managed to walk the whole way home but I felt dirty and used. I went through all the scenarios in my head of how this could play out. I couldn't imagine any plan working out well. If I told someone, it would just create massive, huge embarrassment for everyone. If I told them what happened, I would first have to endure shaming for what I was wearing. She quoted her parents, since *you always dress provocatively, you should cover yourself up.* Then we'd have to go through the public confession of sin—more embarrassment, more shame. In the end, I'm not sure that they would take my side. I got to my home and peered through the window, plotting my path to avoid all conversation, then I bolted for my bedroom."

"What happened next?" George asked, wiping his tears, wanting to wipe hers.

"Thankfully, they were all busy with something and they didn't notice me coming home until mom checked on me later. I told her I was tired, and she left me alone. I can't say that anyone's actions in my family or the church were intentional, but they still didn't help. Over the next few months, I couldn't talk to anyone about what happened fearing it would only make everything worse. Justin noticeably was different. He looked ashamed but never brought himself to apologize. In a few months, he just kind of disappeared from the church. I soldiered on and stuffed down the pain I felt because I couldn't see any practical reason to talk about it—one of those *sleeping dogs*, right?"

"Yeah, but the dogs don't go away; at least that's what I've found," George conceded.

"Exactly, I've found myself raging against some other situation and then realizing this isn't about this situation at all. It's about what happened when I was 16 that never got resolved. That's what I need to get sorted out. I can't keep responding to current situations with my teenage coping mechanisms."

"How do you think *we* can solve it?"

"Well, *we* can't, but *I* have to. A part of me is stuck still being 16. The strategies we have been learning from J.D. and our own struggles to be more whole can work in this situation. Here is what I want to do. I need to speak to *her,* the girl that didn't get to say anything about what happened. So, I need you to not say anything and let me talk to that part of me and let me tell her a few things."

Alesa took the deepest breath, then she began to sob deeply and whispered, "Hello."

For almost five minutes, she just stared at a spot on the wall and turned her head occasionally as though struggling internally. She was silent, but her eyes expressed that care and compassion George knew of her. She would utter short phrases like *I love you* or *I care for you,* or *I see you.* And then her eyes would fill with tears again, and she reached out her arms only to tighten her fists, wrestling with anger, wrestling with pain. Suddenly, she inhaled with her whole body and began slowly addressing her inner child.

"I want you to know that today marks a new day. I remember what happened to you, and it's not your fault. I realize you are a part of me that lives on. We may never forget that day, but it doesn't define us. I feel you when someone gets pushy, but from this point forward when this part of me is triggered, I will have your back. You don't have to be afraid because we can do this together. You are not responsible for what happened to you, and it's okay to feel what you are feeling, just understand that I am older and can help you. And just so you know, I kick ass for breakfast."

"Indeed, you do!" George chimed in, "Oops, I wasn't supposed to speak."

"It's okay," she smiled and continued to take a few deep breaths before opening her eyes and staring into George. She was different now.

He opened his mouth to ask if he could hug her, but she was already moving towards him. As they embraced, they once again felt their hearts beat together. After a few minutes, George opened the outer doors. Ricky brought them some tea. They just looked at each other for a long time, not knowing what to say, but knowing something was better.

George thought about secrets and treasures that night. It didn't make sense, but they were discovering the real treasures that made their life better were always buried in unearthing what they had suppressed. He thought about how different their lives might have been without J.D. and a simple little process to release suppressed feelings. If they ever decided to adopt children, at least the chain of dysfunction might be somewhat disrupted, and his offspring would have a better start. It was one of the hopes he held on to.

After that day, for a couple of years, they could do nothing wrong. Not only were their businesses succeeding, but personally, they were thriving. As the couple felt better personally, they were able to give even more money away to people in need. Some people, like the busybodies, would never be happy, but the couple enjoyed a peace and assurance they were living their best lives.

It was like they were untouchable. Until the sheriff appeared once again.

THE DEATH
(CIRCA 1939-40)

"I HAVE SOME NEWS FOR YOU, POPPER," THE SHERIFF SAID officially. "Your father is dead."

Newly elected Sheriff Tucker was becoming fast friends with the couple. Unlike his predecessor, he ate breakfast nearly every morning in the hotel and soon became popular with most of the employees. He loved hunting and often spent vacations at the sanctuary when things were slow.

His eyes glistened as he continued to stare intently at the couple hoping they would respond soon.

"What? Wait, how did it happen?" George blurted out.

"Well, from what we got, he was going hunting, slipped on the ice, and landed on his back. His shotgun went off, and he was wounded near the back of his head. Your mother found him quickly after she heard the blast, but he was already gone by the time we got there."

George started for the door, but Alesa decided they needed a minute. She called the staff into the dining room and made some quick plans. Alesa would go with Sheriff Tucker and bring Mrs. Popper back to the hotel for a few nights, so she wasn't alone. There was no apparent reason for them to rush out to the homestead now. Hopefully, she would consent to sell it after this, and they could spend some meaningful time with her. Everyone nodded and set out on their assigned missions. George headed for the basement.

He was in a fog as he made his way to the basement. He found his favorite spot where no one could find him. After his last encounter with his dad, he knew that they would probably never speak again, but it still hurt to realize it was over. Part of him grieved. However, he felt relief that now there was closure, a final chapter to their story. He may have wished for a happier ending, but at least now he was sure that wasn't possible. Interestingly, that finality gave him rest.

He took a little while to wonder what happened. It would have been odd for him to have a loaded gun. It just wasn't the normal procedure for hunting to load up until you're ready to shoot. The man had hunted his whole life. To make such a careless mistake was completely out of character. Could he have killed himself? Was he possibly losing his wits in his old age? In the end, George decided to himself that it didn't matter—whether by accident or on purpose. He grappled with this odd mix of emotions, but felt it was best to let it be.

George almost jumped out of his skin when Phillip seemed to magically appear in front of him. He was sure that no one knew his secret hiding spot, but Crazy Phillip did. The noise from above had drowned out the footsteps, and his overconfidence in the security of this spot was his demise.

"How are you, buddy?"

"I'm doing okay. Dad and I weren't close. The last time we spoke, we argued, pretty badly."

"I'm sorry to hear that. Perhaps someday they'll teach dads how to be decent," Phillip consoled.

"I know, right? With all the pressures on people out here on the plains, being a decent father doesn't ever rate high on the priority list. What are you doing down here, and how did you find me?"

"Alesa sent me. She told me where you were and said," holding up his hands in defense, "to get 'your ass' back up there and help her with all the people dropping by."

"People, oh man, I don't want to see people."

"It's so funny, you own a hotel, and you don't like people," Phillip laughed uncontrollably.

"It's not that I don't like people," George defended. "I just don't want to be around them all the time."

"Well, you better get back up there if you know what's good for you."

"Yeah, I know. Let me guess, lots of church people, right? Those bastards are going to start bringing casseroles and sharing the gospel with me. Or they'll tell me *God has a plan* or something else that doesn't help. If they ask me what I remember most, I swear I'm going to say, 'the fact that he was a bastard!'"

"Come on, let's go," Phillip offered George a hand up.

As they climbed the stairs, it occurred to George that life was terribly interesting. A possible former criminal from the city was one of his best friends and most trusted business associates. This "counselor" that changed his personal life was a businessman he didn't know well. If he had the choice, he would gladly swap out his father for Phillip or J.D..

"There he is!" Alesa smiled as the men emerged from the basement.

To George's surprise, there were people everywhere. A line queued out the door for people to say their well wishes to Betty and Alesa. Even more scattered throughout every room on the hotel's first floor. Ricky or someone had put out snacks to satisfy the crowd even though every person coming in was carrying something. This was the good and the bad of small-town life, he thought.

He couldn't help but wonder if some of the people had ulterior motives. However, in the end, they felt the love of the community. Even though a few of the people had some judgments to relay.

The next morning, the couple slept in a little before making sure everything was organized in the packed hotel and heading down to the funeral home. It was a bit awkward when the undertaker talked about his father, descriptions that George could not equate to the man, like caring, loving, and selfless. He tried to just nod his head and let his mom answer any questions. They arranged most of the details, and his parents' church would take care of any service, so George was content with escorting his mother.

They had lunch at the restaurant, but they really didn't talk at all. Both took an afternoon nap which wasn't at all customary. There were different reasons why they weren't talking. For Alesa, she was trying not to say anything harsh. In her mind, George's parents reminded her of her own family's trauma and dysfunction. For George, he always held his mom partially responsible for enabling his dad to be abusive; even though she often comforted him afterward. For his mom, she was miles outside of her element and realizing that she was alone for the first time in her life.

One thing George knew for sure—he and his mom would have to have the conversation they had never been able to have. He knew it might not be today or even next week, but it was going to happen—he could feel it.

The funeral was like every other funeral George had ever been to in his life, only this time he sat in the front pew. There were several songs by a couple of the busybodies slightly off-key accompanied by a piano player that must have been aged a century. Like most church services, Alesa and George both had triggers from their individual experiences. Some things stoked fond memories and others resurrected nightmares.

George thought about those awkward things people say when someone dies. But this funeral was the worst of everything. The pastor attempted to say positive things about the deceased, scanning the church for validation. However, the congregation stared at the floor avoiding the guilting glare of the pastor. The reception afterward lasted forever, and they had thanked practically every person in town, even the busybodies.

Some in George's situation might wish to bring their parents back to have those precious "last words." But they had already said their peace, so it was cathartic when George and Alesa left for home and to their own lives. The relationship with mom might have a chance, but they were happy regardless. After the charade was over that day, they felt better and not at all guilty.

"Mom, what are you going to do?" George said abruptly in the car.

"Let's talk when we get to the hotel," she said. "I have much to say."

"Oh hell," he said, "you know I love to talk!"

She just laughed. They all snuck glances at each other on the way home. Surprisingly, they all were somber but peaceful. Alesa mentioned that she was glad they didn't have to stand at the pulpit coming up with filler words said after someone dies to make others feel better. George and his mom nodded their heads like they were cut from the same cloth.

"Why don't you live with us," George said abruptly, as Alesa shot him a cold, hard stare.

This violated the *we-didn't-talk-about-this-first* rule, and he knew he was in trouble. But something in him connected with his mother, and he wanted to see if they could build something.

"Like I said, let's talk at the hotel," she said calmly.

A BOY AND HIS MOM

"I SHOT HIM," SHE CONFESSED BEFORE THEY EVEN SAT down at the table.

George just fell silent. After some time, he raised an eyebrow, and she nodded once with a confidence he had never seen in her. George glanced around only to see Alesa frozen in the corner, hand over mouth. He looked at the woman who raised him, the woman who gave him life. She repeated her nod. He slowly leaned back in the chair.

"That's right. I shot that son-of-a-bitch in the back of the head. I'm not a bit sorry. Even before you came out to talk, he has been getting meaner and meaner the last few years. The sheriff knows I shot him. I could see it in his eyes. But he just agreed with whatever I said. The violence just kept getting worse. I couldn't take it anymore. Right before, I said, 'I want to move to town.' You know what he said? He told me, 'You'll do what I tell you.' And just like that, I was done. I snapped. I took his daddy's old over-under off the mantle and shot him while he was walking away from me."

"I tried to get him to say he was sorry," George mumbled, taking it all in. "He just wouldn't."

"He was sorry about a lot of things, but he couldn't say it. It's how we lived. Take care of the food, the farm, the kids. We were supposed to care about those trivial things, but those are what mattered! We just didn't have time for it, and we never learned how to say the things we needed to say. When you went to the Army, you broke those patterns and that lovely woman of yours taught you some new practices that have made you a better man. I'm so happy for you kids, but I was stuck. Even the church turned a blind eye because I was supposed to be *obedient* or *submissive* to him. I never bought it, but he believed it. He *relied* on it."

Alesa couldn't stand to the side any longer. She walked straight to her mother-in-law, knelt, took both her hands, and drew her into a tight hold. Betty stiffened at first to the intimate touch, but then opened and accepted the embrace. Both cried for several minutes. When they released each other, they took a moment to wipe tears and even smile. When Alesa sat down next to George, she patted his leg, encouraging him to go on. George had composed himself enough to speak.

"So, what do you want to do now? I guess you're not going to jail. What do you want to do with the rest of your life? What can we do to make your dreams come true?"

"I want you to give me a job in the hotel, wherever you see fit. Then I just want a room with a nice bed. I want someone to sell the homestead and everything on it except for a few knickknacks I'll pick out. With whatever time I have left, I'd like you guys to take me on a couple of vacations each year until I die. How about that?"

"That sounds achievable," Alesa's smile broadened.

"So, we have a loose plan?" George chuckled. Clearly, his mother had held this dream in secret for a long time.

Like many other things that happened at the hotel, this discussion had begun with the most unusual circumstances. Part of the reason they were happy was because they had somehow accepted that the circumstances of life are very rarely ideal. George's dad never understood this. He spent his whole life trying to wrangle life to fit his expectations and ideals, and life chose not to cooperate in that way. The fear of losing control causes people to make extreme choices. Mom, Alesa, and George subconsciously agreed that daring adventures are more significant than scripted plans.

"How about you bring me a drink," Betty said.

"One step ahead of you," Ricky said, coming out of nowhere. "Try this wine I've been saving for a special occasion."

For the rest of the night, Mom (as everyone started calling her) talked like they had never seen her talk. It was as if her voice had been bottled up for decades. She told stories about George and his siblings. She talked about politics and movies she wanted to see. Most of those that wandered by the restaurant table truly noticed her for the first time. They could see the resemblance to George and George's passion in this woman. All that he had hoped for was blooming in this moment.

George just watched her and marveled at all she said and how she made them laugh. George was already secure in his place in the world, and he was comfortable being who he was. But now he had a bonus. Now, he had his mom again! He imagined her baking her famous blueberry muffins and tending to the flower beds. And maybe, just maybe, they would talk some more.

The next morning, George and Betty had breakfast in the restaurant. It was a luxury her father would never accommodate even after they had plenty of money. She ordered almost one of everything without remorse and ate like a hungry teenager before leaning back and realizing how she must have appeared. But she just laughed.

"Whew!" Betty giggled, "I can't remember the last time I ate food that someone else cooked. That was so wonderful!" She cocked her head toward George. "Son, do you know that I am proud of you?"

"I do. I have always known that."

"But it's not just the money and success. You and that little lady and figured out some secrets to being happy. Lots of people are wealthy. Very few people are genuinely happy."

"I've thought about writing some of this stuff down … like a secret to life book or something."

"That sounds great!" Mom said.

"What about your church?" George questioned.

"I told them at the funeral, I'm not coming back. I believe in God and find the way of Christ compelling, but everything is so oppressive. We all must agree. We all must support the group, so we can pay the pastor to tell us what to think. It stopped making sense a long time ago. I like listening to people have discussions about God, but I don't want to go to a bible study to train me how to think like them. Every chance I get, I latch on to books which expand my mind and help me think *bigger*. I guess church became a confining box instead of an enlightened pathway. In the early days, when it was all new, it was exciting, but hasn't been for a long time."

"That is very close to how I feel," George stated.

"People think when you state things like this, it means you hate God, or you are against the church. But that's not it. I just want to grow and discover, and I think that's alright. Nevertheless, most of them will not speak to me now. I am threatening them because entertaining these types of ideas threatens to dislodge their certainty. And that is something they can't have."

George realized he was a lot like his mom. He admired her strength but knew that she was so much like Alesa that he briefly wondered if they would butt heads. He smiled knowing they most definitely would, but it would be okay, and they would get through it.

"I want to go out for a walk, but I don't want anyone to come with me," she blurted out.

"Okay, but why?"

"It's just the first time in forever that I have been free. I want to be myself, go where I want to go, see what I want to see, and potentially buy what I want to buy. I don't want anyone to tell me what to do, and if they do, I'm going to tell them what is."

George just burst out laughing before giving his mom a side-ways glance.

"I'm serious, you better warn your townspeople that Betty is about to come to town!" she said, as she looked around the room for supporters.

Several others caught on and joined in their frivolity.

George never took lightly what they knew about the shooting. They still considered it somewhat wrong, but the lesser of two evils. It was like self-defense by a slave that was controlled their whole life. When the one in charge progressively got more violent, it seemed like the only way out. It caused a dilemma with her old religion, but it wasn't the only conflict she knew. Like everyone they had good days and bad days wrestling with the challenges of life.

Fortunately, George and Alesa were able to *focus* with her and help her face some trauma that had been long inside. By visiting the trauma, she was able to nurture her inner wounds and shift that "stuck" mentality. She never went to jail, but she did rehabilitate, and she did leave an indelible mark in the world. From that day forward, every person she touched called her *mom* for the rest of her life. She may have left religion, but she always said that she *found love* and to her that was God.

For George and Alesa, it was like something was re-attached to them that should have already been there. They weren't necessarily resentful of the past, but they were overtly thankful for what was happening now, and they made the most of it.

ONE MORE TRY
AT THE HOTEL

It took several attempts for Joe to connect with Marla. Winter always slowed things down in smaller towns. It seemed to take so much more time getting around in wintry weather and, worse, getting out of bed at all. Joe was still interested in the part of the hotel he had not yet seen. It was where Marla believed the car was buried. Even the question of *Why did she think this?* begged to be answered.

As he trudged through the snow, he couldn't help but remember when snow was a once in a lifetime occurrence that usually and quickly dissipated. He was now well-accustomed to walking effectively in the snow and even owned some snow boots that he never had out at the right time. Navigating winter and the snow was a normal part of his existence now.

"Good morning, friend," he said, walking up the steps and instinctively shaking the powdery remnants from his shoes.

"It's sure coming down, isn't it?" Marla remarked, referring to the precipitation.

"Indeed," Joe replied, wondering why it was mandatory to talk about the weather even though he was sure that was his default as well.

"How's the research coming?" Marla inquired.

"It's frustrating at times, and I get sidetracked. I don't know if we'll ever find anything earth-shattering that the locals don't already know, but I feel like a better person. I think I'm growing and healing, as odd as that sounds."

"Most things are like that," Marla said, taking the tone of the local sage.

"What I would like to see next, as we have talked about, is the first floor and basement I haven't seen. You said your husband has tools on the first floor, and you don't want people in there, but how do we get to the basement? It exists but doesn't exist. Know what I mean?"

"Well, I can show you the first floor," Marla said. "My husband gave me permission."

The entrance to the ballroom was toward the back of the hotel. As he crossed the threshold, he was once again surprised. Everything was covered in dust and looked aged, but this was truly a magnificent room. The walls were ornately decorated, and the dual chandeliers were obviously beyond the norm for anything in this area. Marla's husband's tools were scattered across the back side of the ballroom, but the grandeur of the room won out.

Marla took him to the back corner and let him take it all in from another angle.

"Wow, this is stunning!" Joe said. "Truly amazing."

His eyes were drawn up to the crown molding that was obviously from a different period. It reminded him of his 1920s house and the woodwork that was there. It would be almost impossible now to find a craftsman that had the time and patience to create such beautiful ornamentation. Lighting was limited so Joe moved around trying to get a better view. It was then that he tripped over the loose flooring. Embarrassed, he jogged toward the front of the room taking note of the stage and dance floor and the dated furniture pushed up against the front wall.

Marla was fixed at the back of the room so eventually, when his curiosity was satisfied, he returned to her side only to trip over the same flooring again and fell to his knees. He turned to see exactly what it was he stumbled upon.

"What is that?" he pointed, irritated and still embarrassed.

"Oh, I don't know," Marla said almost playfully.

He looked at her for too long. They barely knew each other, but in a way, they were partners in this endeavor. Like most people, he sometimes trusted her and at other times, he wondered if she was just playing some angle on him. He was usually childishly optimistic and reluctantly cautious. Currently, he was excited!

"It's a piece of plywood ... brand-new plywood. Care if I move it?"

"Sure, I'm not exactly positive what it is, but he's been uncovering a lot of stuff back in this area."

Once again, he studied her face, not sure of anything at this point.

The plywood wasn't even secured, it was just covering up something. As he investigated, he could see evidence that a stud wall had once surrounded this area. Except for the missing walls and the odd positioning, it seemed like where a staircase could be.

"No way!" he said as he lifted the plywood and leaned it against the wall, almost falling into the hole it covered.

"I've never seen this before," Marla once again non-convincingly protested.

"Is that a hole or a—" Joe paused to click his new flashlight.

"Oh my," Marla said again, not that convincingly.

"Can I go down there?" Joe said like a boy outside a candy store Christmas display.

The stairs leading downstairs were surprisingly sturdy and simple. This was not a public entrance. Since the steps were uneven and unfinished, Joe assumed this was not constructed by the same people that built the ballroom above and refinished the rest of the hotel. His assumption immediately was that these stairs might have been constructed by George himself. After almost falling a couple times, he completed his journey down the makeshift stairs.

There was a fair amount of dust, but since the room was essentially sealed from all sides, it was relatively undisturbed. From what he was learning about the hotel, he quickly recognized the room as the speakeasy where party goers would come to escape attention and enjoy themselves during the tough times of the era. Unlike the other areas of the hotel, this area was not cluttered, it had an eerie orderliness to it that was different.

Marla stayed upstairs, staying consistent to her aversion to things subterranean.

"You knew about this, didn't you?" he bellowed up the stairs.

"Perhaps" she said, allowing him to explore with an open mind.

"Okay, just give me some time. This is a lot to take in."

Joe moved methodically slowly around the room. He remembered his days playing video games and searching for treasure. He would keep moving in one direction through all the twists and turns until he eventually arrived back at where he started. He wasn't sure whether it was okay, but he took pictures of everything, every single *piece of evidence* is what he called it in his mind.

Every piece of furniture fit the motif of a speakeasy bar, but on every surface, there were remnants from many time periods. There were awards with George Popper's name, but also pictures and various trinkets that had some significance simply because of the way they were displayed.

On the first side wall, he almost missed them because his eyes were focused lower on the assortment of displays. There were more shovels, only these were much more preserved, and it only took a slight dusting to see what they were. They were in honor of all the business started by the Poppers and/or J.D. Enterprises. It was like a trophy case on the wall. Moving from left to right, he recognized the sanctuary, the gun shop, and several other businesses that he heard mentioned from time-to-time. Several of them he couldn't even understand since they just had the title of the business and "Congratulations," and a date … and a signature of sorts, "J.D. Morelli."

As he moved past the last shovel, he also noticed something that made him gasp. There were exactly two hooks and two obvious spots for the missing shovels. He knew where those shovels were, but he still had more questions about why they were moved and why they eventually got hidden inside the walls in other places.

On the front wall, there was an assortment of liquor bottles which appeared to be full and undisturbed. These might have some monetary value, but the appearance was this was a display of a private collection. By now, he was guessing this collection of random, memorable items was the collection of George Popper. At one time, alcohol was a precious commodity, and word on the street was that the hotel had a special supplier that could get anything for the right price.

Piled in one of the booths was another collection of memorabilia. He sat for half an hour carefully examining each article. Most of it was old and dusty but caused him to smile. There were pictures, collectibles, and documents. As he examined each item, he paused briefly to retrofit each item into his story about the hotel. Some things fit well, and others created new questions. These things were the missing parts to the story that he was searching for in the library.

He stood up, and turned away from this wall briefly to rub his eyes and take a deep breath. Walking above had disturbed some dust on the rafters, but that was all just beginning to settle, and he saw it! It wasn't a car, it was a truck! This relic of the past was in mint condition. He took just a step toward it, not wanting to abandon his working plan to search the walls for clues. It was beautiful, but how did they get it down here?

For the moment, he left the treasure parked on the dance floor and continued his search. Eventually, he entered what was once a storeroom, which was not wholly empty. As he exited the storeroom, he noticed the mirrored back wall of the bar area. Where the liquor normally would be was covered mostly by random pictures of events in the hotel, celebrities, and more awards from various times including George Popper's time in the army.

As he turned around, George noticed the original cash register, and he couldn't help but pull the arm down to open it. No cash remained, of course, but it made him feel satisfied to look. Scanning for a safe below led his eyes to the document shelves which were most logically for storing record books, mail, and other necessary business items. They too were empty, except for one narrow shelf with a folder slightly exposed. Joe reached down and carefully removed it. It was a manuscript!

As he removed layers of dust, he slowly deciphered the title on the outside. It read:

What Life is All About by George Popper

It was hand dated, but the last number wasn't clear. It was either 1943, 1946, or 1948. Joe was so excited! This not only was this a revealing insight into the former hotel owner, but was also exactly the kind of thing he would be interested in reading.

He passed over the restrooms and several more tables of memorabilia. As he took one last glance at the room before heading upstairs, he summarized the room as something like a museum of history. Although there were no labels on anything, it was obvious what most things were. It was one man's time capsule which was sealed for his own reflection and was meant only to be found posthumously. Heading up the stairs, he noticed the over/under shotgun leaning into a corner which made him only slightly pause before calling out to Marla.

"Hey, look what I found," he began. "Listen, I know you guys have seen this room. I could see footprints and you're not a particularly good liar. I know you have reasons for keeping people out of here, but this is something special." As he displayed the manuscript to her, he couldn't withhold his excitement.

"What is it?"

"It's a manuscript by George Popper. "

"That's amazing! We must have missed it. We're always focused on restoration and cleaning and sometimes we overlook those little tidbits that don't look important. We missed the shovel for over a year."

"Can I take it home?" Joe offered. "I'll make copies and store it digitally. I promise I'll take good care of it. This may be the treasure we were looking for."

She thought a while but agreed. As they were walking out, something passed in front of them. They both felt it and stopped for a second.

"Did you feel that?" Marla said.

Joe just nodded his head, and they just stood still for a second only to hear a creak on the stairs to the basement. Their experiences before kept them from being afraid. It was more like intrigue and curiosity. For the first time in decades the time capsule was disturbed, and Joe carried the manuscript, the manifesto, of whatever that likely inhabited this place.

"Wow!" they both said at the same time. They waited a few moments more, maybe to see if George was coming to claim his book.

"I'll see you soon. I'll upload this and email you a PDF," Joe said, almost falling down the front steps in his careless excitement.

The streets were a little clearer than before. This would make it easier to navigate the hill to his home. As the car warmed up, he thought through the events of today. He thought about George's advice to *let it come* to him and the mantra he grew up with to *go make it happen*. He proposed that it must be a combination of both. The treasures of the world, like the manuscript, don't necessarily find you sitting at home, but they do come to you as you are going. While in his mind he imagined things like money and other material treasures, what he found may have been even better—you must seek to find, but maybe it's better not to know what you are looking for.

He knew Mary would be curious. There was a certain amount of debrief after every adventure. He was excited to tell her, but he knew he would be required to fill in some details and not just jump to the climax of the story. So, he tucked the manuscript safely away in his backpack and headed into his home.

He glanced at his phone just in time to see a note that she was taking a nap, and subsequently, entered quietly. He very soon fell asleep in his chair thinking about the truck on the dance floor only to awaken quickly wondering if it was all a dream. Joe checked his backpack and patted the folder with the manuscript before falling back onto his pillow.

"You gonna sleep all day?" Mary whispered to him.

"Ha-ha. I had quite the experience today. Finally got in the basement. It's like a museum!"

She caught on to what he was doing and cut him off at the pass. He was trying to summarize everything, and she wanted details. She was better at steering him in the right direction than he was dodging her direction, so he explained the whole experience up to and including the encounter with George or whatever that was at the end.

"So, this manuscript … it's like a manifesto?" she questioned.

"Well, to tell you the truth, I didn't want to read until I was ready. It is like a big deal, and I wanted to read it to you. I know, I'm a fabulous guy, and you can thank me later."

They both chuckled a little, and she gave him a playful *watch it, mister* look.

"Later tonight, after supper, let's prepare for it and take it all in together."

"Is this going to be our new religion?" she teased. "You're not going to start a new church!"

"Maybe," he lobbed back, "we can call ourselves Poppers."

"Okay, I'll make some spaghetti while we're watching the news, then later we will learn what life *is* all about. Sounds like we're all set!"

For a while, they were engrossed in the barrage of strife the media played out in between commercials for medications they couldn't pronounce and shows they never watched until they couldn't take it anymore and shut off the tv. Mary chose to light a few candles and settle into their seat in their modest living room. Joe took Gaston out, so that wouldn't be an issue, and hid his ball so he wouldn't decide to play right in the middle of it.

"What if this is not any good?" Joe worried.

"It'll be great! Let's get to it ... read to me, stud!"

A SURPRISING RETURN
(CIRCA 1952)

GEORGE ATE A LATE SUNDAY BRUNCH WITH RICKY. THEY had become close friends over the years. Like many successful people, George realized that he had very few close friends. But Ricky was one of the few people that knew him well and told him the truth. Alesa was the same type of friend in addition to being his spouse. He now also considered his mother a friend after the reconciliation they experienced in recent years. These three friends were enough for him although he missed J.D. still.

"I have a few things to add to your collection downstairs," Ricky said.

"How do you know about the downstairs?" George questioned.

"You should know by now, that nothing is a secret around here. We're like a tight-knit, dysfunctional family. It's okay, everyone knows that is your place and not to mess with it, but we also know how to get in there if we want."

"What are the things you want to add?"

"I have some old menus in pristine condition and the awards the restaurant got and our cookbooks. I have mint condition copies of all that stuff."

"Sure, put it all in a box. Or, I guess, just take it down there yourself," George smiled.

The two of them were finishing up their meals when a sort of commotion broke out at the front of the hotel. Both looked up when Alesa appeared in the doorway, eyes wide, and motioned them forward.

They walked slowly, but directly out into the lobby, and immediately they saw what the fuss was about.

"Look, it's J.D.," Alesa yelled out.

"I can see that," George mouthed quietly as he continued to move forward.

Several employees were hugging the hotel's prodigal father and enthusiastically welcoming him back. As the crowd began to thin, Alesa and George moved closer and embraced him at the same time. He was immaculately dressed, as always, but something about him seemed a bit frailer.

"What are you doing? How are you here?" Alesa blurted out.

"We'll talk a little later," J.D. said. "Could someone get me a glass of water?"

The couple ushered him out of the diminishing crowd, and they all kept looking at each other. It was as if they were getting acquainted again without any words. They remembered why they loved each other, all the memories resurfacing instantaneously. They were eternally connected, but their physical connection had waned while J.D. was in prison.

"Listen, they let me out a little early, but I'd like to talk to the two of you more privately."

"I need to go do a couple of important errands, but I'll be back in about an hour," Alesa said, hugging him tightly and backing away trying to take it all in.

"I want to show you something new. Follow me." George gushed.

The two of them moved toward the back of the room, toward the bigger ballroom, and then toward the hidden stairway down to the basement and his now not-so-secret place. J.D.'s gait was slower than before. He had a slight limp and winced occasionally. Ricky popped up with a carafe of water, a couple of glasses, and some water crackers and fresh cheddar. George studied his friend taking in the subtle changes in J.D.'s appearance as both fondly replayed their history.

"This is my new place. Watch your step. I crafted the stairs myself."

"Oh, you're about as good of a carpenter as you are a cook." J.D. said, chuckling to himself before steadying his hand on the wall, looking down at treacherous steps.

"I'm actually a very competent cook. people just don't appreciate spice here in these parts."

J.D. scanned all the additions to the room. He was familiar with what had been the old speakeasy but was taken aback by all the additional items carefully placed around the walls. Most of them were familiar as he nodded and pointed, inspecting each. But, when he saw the truck in the middle of the room, he laughed heartily and shook his head at George.

"How the hell did you get that down here?"

"Actually, it was Phillip. It was something to see!"

"Is that your dad's truck?"

"Yes! It was the one he bought before his death. It was the only thing he ever *splurged on. I wanted to find the wagon, but it is long gone.*"

"Why would you want to keep it?" J.D. asked, looking concerned.

"Because of what you taught me. You can't heal unless you face it and feel it. I have faced it and felt it and now I am better. I've even cleared the air with my mom, who lives here by the way. This truck is the biggest reminder I could imagine that ignoring things never makes anything better. And it's a beautiful truck anyway. I always loved it, even if I hated him."

J.D. didn't say anything but just nodded in agreement. The two of them stared at each other and the truck for a few more minutes. The basement was cool and comfortable. All the exits had been sealed up, including the tunnel that used to bring not only customers and traffic, but also smells and sounds from the outside. The only sound now was the small exhaust fan and occasional footsteps from the group setting up for a wedding upstairs.

"Let me tell you why I am here," J.D. suddenly turned to George. "I was released early from prison because of good behavior and … because I don't have long to live," he raised his hand to protest George's shock and fear. "The cancer is in my vital organs, and I just needed to do two things before I go home to die. I wanted to visit my relatives like Phillip, who I saw already, and to visit my two best friends, you and Alesa."

George was touched. As he reflected earlier, successful people don't have that many devoted friends, and he was honored that J.D. considered him in his small group. He couldn't articulate how they came to this arrangement, but he was grateful for this special friend. He tried not to hold things against his father, but he acknowledged that his father wouldn't even drive to town to visit his son because of their relationship. Because of this, he appreciated the commitment of J.D. to their friendship and business relationship.

"What is the motivation for this place?" he asked his younger friend.

"I can't explain it except that I think it's helpful to remember. You can't live in the past, but it's necessary to go there occasionally. It helps me be grateful, and it helps me heal in some cases. I also want to preserve some things to help tell the story. I guess I can explain it after all."

"You certainly can," J.D. said proudly. "I think it's great! I must ask, though. What happened to two of the shovels that are missing from the wall?"

"I meant to talk to Phillip about those when I saw them the other day. Both were misplaced when incidents happened in this room. You know how people pick up pool cues when a fight breaks out. It's sort of the same thing with those shovels. Every time people got heated, which wasn't *that* often, people would grab one of them. Most times, their friends would stop them before it got out of hand, but a couple of times there was blood on these shovels. It was back in the days of the busybodies and that crazy sheriff, so to be safe we just got rid of them."

"So, did anyone get killed?" J.D. ask, clearing his throat.

"We don't even know because most times the friends just get them out quickly. But I don't think so. It's just a couple of situations that went too far, so we hid the shovels but I'm not sure where Phillip put them. I trust him."

"I hid them in a wall," Phillip said from the top-level of the steps.

They turned around quickly, mouths wide open. None of them knew he was there or for sure that he knew how to get down there. The stairway was supposed to be a secret entrance.

"I guess everyone knows how to get here. We should just reopen to the public," George sadly mentioned. He liked having a private place to go to, but it never quite worked out like he imagined.

"George, I'm so proud of you!" J.D. said without warning, "you've succeeded in business, but you have also progressed in dealing with your demons and facing your *shadow* issues. Very few people do either one of those things long term. I think you should write all this stuff down."

"That means a lot coming from you because I attribute most of my success and healing to you."

"But you did something with it!" J.D. emphasized. "I hope you write it all down for the next owner."

"Funny you should mention it. My mother told me almost the exact same thing after my father died, and I've been writing it down ever since. Alesa has been typing it up for me. Every time I learn something new, I've been putting it in the folder."

"Can I see it?" J.D. asked hopefully.

George walked over to the counter and brought the folder to his friends. He almost reluctantly handed it off, careful not to wrinkle the parchment. J.D. at once read it, greedily devouring each word like it was his last meal. He leaned into the manuscript to see it closely as his eyesight was now drastically failing him along with his health. Several times, George tried to explain something in the manuscript, but the older friend just held up his hand and kept reading. Eventually, he finished and closed the folder. Both noticed Alesa's presence behind them.

"I like two things about it. The title and everything in it. This is exactly what I would write if I had your gift or more time. I would say that every young person should read it, but those who aren't ready to hear this won't learn anything at all. So, I wish you well sharing it with others. Just know that this and all this," he gesticulated towards the manuscript and George's private space, "is great!"

"So, what do you want? What can we do for you that would make you happy?" Alesa asked.

"It's quite simple. I want to spend a couple of days at the sanctuary in a cabin that faces the evening sun. Then, my associate will come get me and take me home to rest. I won't have any kind of funeral, so this is your last chance to say goodbye. As you know, all my assets have been split up—what is left of my living expenses will be given to my favorite charity. That's it! I'm done! If there's an afterlife, I'll see ya there. But, either way, I think I'll haunt this place whenever I damn well please."

He started to laugh, but a coughing spurt cut it short. Alesa and George teared up and gathered around him briefly before they silently made their way upstairs. He talked with every employee in the hotel for hours before giving his associate the nod, and they moved toward the door. George and Alesa hugged and watched their dear friend quietly pass out of their lives.

The following morning, the caretakers were waiting for them at breakfast, but they knew what had happened. J.D. died in his sleep, and his driver had taken him away without ceremony. They reported he was happy, but tired and laid down and gave up his fight.

George and Alesa took a walk that morning. They didn't say anything. Both occasionally looked like they were going to say something then would cry. They kept altering their route to avoid people, so they could remember their good friend. Every object in nature would remind them about aspects of J.D.'s personality or things that he once said.

Nancy bought some flowers downtown and placed them on the counter in the hotel. Mom kept fresh flowers in the vase for years after his death. Alesa and George traditionally touched the vessel every morning and paused for a brief second, usually with a whispered *miss you* or *love you, friend.*

The couple started a scholarship in his name which exists to this day.

WHAT LIFE IS ALL ABOUT

JOE BEGAN READING TO MARY. HE CLEARED HIS THROAT because he wasn't a natural speaker and needed to speak up to be heard. His spouse had a slight challenge with her hearing, so it probably would have been better the other way, but he felt like it required a man's voice to read what a man wrote.

WHAT LIFE IS ALL ABOUT
by George Popper

I was surprised when my mom said I should write this because I have never been a writer. She thinks I am successful at life, and I agree with her. We succeeded financially, and also, we have been fortunate to discover some healing methods from friends like J.D. Morelli and others.

I feel like the luckiest person in the world, but it wasn't just luck that propelled us forward. There are some principles that worked. Violating the truths holds us back and following them helps us achieve more.

In this document, I will try to articulate what I have learned from my life running a hotel with my wife and navigating the ups and downs of what I consider a life well-lived.

My father was the son of an immigrant, so my life started out at somewhat of a disadvantage, and my home life was far from perfect. I was able to meet the love of my life,

Alesa, after I finished a short tour in the Army. She is
the number one reason why I am successful, and the rest
of this explanation follows suit to that initial fact. But
most people say that about their spouse, so I will continue on with what I promised my mom I would do.

1. What is not felt cannot heal.

A long time ago, my friend J.D. shared something painful with me about his past. He wasn't telling me what he
"thought" about it; he was telling me what he felt. This
was painful for him to do, but when he did it, something
changed inside him, and he felt better afterwards.

I have come to understand that most of us are traumatized. I was abused by my father. My wife was injured by
her parents' personalities and something too personal
for me to tell you. Both of us have some trauma from
religious experiences, and almost everyone I know has
been negatively affected by something.

But just because most people have past hurt, doesn't mean
that we should ignore it because ignoring things almost
never helps them get better.

When traumatizing things happen, and we don't know
how to deal with them, it creates what Carl Jung called
"shadow" within. Several of the people associated with
the hotel read some literature from the psychoanalyst
and started to understand this better. If we keep stuff-
ing these things down, eventually they come out sideways.
It's like when we blow up for no good reason. We are using
the coping strategies we had at the time of the trauma.

I would encourage anyone to find a therapist or someone
that understands this process. But above all else, ask
for help. We experience this trauma through experience,

so we have to process it the same way. We think of it like talking to our inner child and our inner critic. These processes are new and not a lot of people understand them.

If we just keep ignoring our pain, we will only be surviving and not thriving.

Some parts of being successful are hard work. I hired people to work for me, but I also had to work hard to make sure everything ran well and was organized. In a similar way, becoming more whole is also hard work. In most cases, it involves asking for help. If we don't give up, we can usually get to a better place within ourselves. I suspect that most success is not about what happens outside, but inside. I don't go to church much, but Jesus said, "The Kingdom of God is within you."

Alesa and I have both done some hard work dealing with our trauma. It wasn't easy, but it was worth it.

In this town, they say "let sleeping dogs lie," but we have discovered that things very rarely get better by doing nothing. We may forget them for a time, but they don't go away. Our bodies want to resolve the things that never got resolved.

We have helped several people face their trauma and get better, just like someone helped us. I hope everyone will get this help before they traumatize others. I believe cycles can be broken and family trees can be changed if people will give inner work the attention it deserves.

2. Life is not ideal; it is messy.

I used to wish that life would be better. What I meant by that is I wanted life to behave and act the way I

expected it to. But life never conformed to my expectations. It did what it wanted to do. Principles helped me
effectively respond to circumstances, but circumstances
could rarely be predicted.

The harder I tried to wrangle life to fit my agenda, the
more problems I created for myself. The more I accepted
that life was unpredictable and messy, the more I could
adjust to the obstacles it presented.

We wanted life to be an adventure, but eventually we
learned that adventures can't be scripted. In fact, by
definition an adventure goes against order and predict-
ability. So, if we want a true journey, we have to open up
to the chaotic nature of life and pay attention to what's
going on when the itinerary of life changes.

There were so many times when circumstances changed
and at first, I was afraid that I couldn't control the
situation. Then, suddenly, I realized that I was on an
adventure and began to notice the multi-colored scenery
that I was missing.

Most of our success was during prohibition and the panic.
There were attacks from people that wanted us to fail.
One of our sheriffs was out to get me because I beat him
at wrestling earlier in life. Actually, it was a tie—but
he saw it as a defeat. There were weather challenges and
family issues and difficult guests. All these things
made up the tapestry of our experience. They weren't
bumps in the road or detours to our journey—they were
the actual journey.

At some point, I realized it was my fear that was driving
my need to control. When I stopped trying to excessively
manage my life, life became a lot more vivid and exciting. I was still responsible, but I didn't have to script
everything in advance.

Eventually I learned not to say, "it shouldn't be like this," and started to say, "I wasn't expecting this, but this is what it is." When I could be where I was with the things that were, then I could also start to live in that situation more authentically. In a way, being where I was, helped me to be who I was.

Life is not ideal, it's an adventure—lean into it!

3. Some thoughts about religion.

As I said before, I don't go to church. My family was Christian, but there are lots of triggers for both Alesa and I. We were always working on Sunday, and it just never made sense to us to sit and listen to someone telling us what we should think. I don't begrudge anyone that finds a home there. I wish you well.

My feeling is that religion is people trying to understand God. It always has been that. It is seeking after God to try to understand. Men and women have searched and reasoned and written holy books to try to make sense of this God we can't see. Sometimes men have even made idols of the books or the people of the religion or their particular group.

But ultimately religion is man-made and sometimes inspired.

I personally find some things Jesus said very compelling. When he talked about loving your neighbor and enemies and then later said to treat people like you want to be treated, I can get on board with those ideas. Mercy, grace, compassion, forgiveness are all things that make the world better.

But for me, it's also important to keep an open mind. There are other teachers (like the Buddha) that also taught valuable lessons, and I learn just as much about God from nature as I do from a preacher. So, I don't want to limit myself just to Christianity, and especially not just one narrow view of that faith. As long as I am still asking questions and searching, I have the possibility of learning and expanding my consciousness.

Speaking of other teachers, Carl Jung believed in a collective unconscious that we share with other members of the human race which also includes memories of our "ancestral and evolutionary past."

If anyone finds this manuscript and reads it in the future, hopefully, they will have figured some of this stuff out already and they will have evolved to the point of being less angry about being right all the time.

I can't imagine that a God that is so hard to figure out would be as angry as we are that we can't do a better job of understanding him or her or it. After all this time, we haven't really got much clarity, yet we often are absolutely certain about our ambiguity. I personally see this as ridiculous.

I hope the people that come after me will be grateful for what they feel and know inside about God, but that they will come to a peace about what they don't understand and where they disagree. Then, they can all search together and discover the unbelievable value of adventure and the mystery and nuance and paradox in it all.

For a time, I had a secret place in my basement where I could hide and just think for a while. One day, I saw a sunflower seed on the floor and I just stopped for a moment to think about that seed. With a little water and a little time, that seed will start to grow into a giant plant. So, within the seed is all the energy and intelligence to grow into a full-grown plant. It's mind-boggling to think about such things.

When Jesus says, "the Kingdom of God is within you," what if he meant that God is in all things? Perhaps God is like energy and intelligence which seem to be in every-thing. The bird outside my window is building a nest—who taught her to do that?

So, for me, my religion is the wonder and wandering to discover the absolute beauty and brilliance of every-thing I see, from the complexity of the human brain to the simple majesty in a flower that my mother tended. They possess energy and intelligence and their own form of beauty and majesty.

To me, God is in everything, and it makes no sense to confine myself to a building once a week, when I can dis-cover all this out here, in everyone and in everything. If it makes sense to other people to do it in their own way, then so be it. They deserve to be happy in whatever way they choose, but I don't think God is prescribing everything that they think.

One more thing—most religions are initially based on fear. I don't think that's necessary. Even the Christian Bible commands quite often, "Don't fear." Fear causes peo-ple to want to control, and as I said before, trying to control life doesn't work out well. So, even if people have to have an organized religion, I encourage them to not try to control it. Good luck with that!

4. Paul was wrong; women are equals.

Some people treat the Apostle Paul like he was God. He had some unique revelations, but he never actually met

Jesus in person. Most of the sore spots are that Western Christianity has designed a lot of their rules of assembly from Paul's suggestions. An example of this would be that women should be silent in church.

I want to say something crass at this point, but that wouldn't be loving my neighbor, would it?

Without interpreting any Greek or doing any complex, systematic theology, I just want to say that Paul was wrong about several issues. It doesn't mean that he can't be in the Bible or be respected. Other authors in the Book were wrong about things, and they can still be viewed as people on the journey trying to understand God, and like us, they still didn't understand everything perfectly.

Women are capable of doing almost everything men can do. My mother was silenced by the church and her husband for most of her life. After his untimely death, she blossomed into one of the most beloved people in our community. When she spoke up and had her own ideas and even taught others, she affected almost everyone she met.

Alesa is basically the CEO of our hotel. She and I talk about most decisions, but she is the boss, and she makes it run. When I resent this or try to let the Apostle Paul tell us how to run a business, I only have problems. I suppose that might be part of the issues in the church—we have missed half the sermons we should have heard because women have been so muted and ignored.

I hope this situation changes sometime in the future. Women now can vote, so the sky's the limit. Hopefully soon, it will not be that uncommon for a woman to run a church or a bank or even be the sheriff. We have done our part to set an example, and I couldn't be happier about it.

Again, it boils down to fear and control. If we don't start out lamenting about what might happen, we wouldn't try to control it so much that we hurt its effectiveness. Our hotel was known for being the best hotel in a hundred miles largely because the right person was in charge.

Using that number, I hope in 2020 (100 years from when women got the right to vote) that women will be seen in even the highest office in the land. Maybe I'm a dreamer, but dreams are where realities begin.

5. The real treasure is in you.

People always seem to be searching for lost treasure. I guess it's the inclination people have to get something for nothing. It's rare that they ever find it, but they will search for it until they find something or waste all their money.

People come to the hotel to get away. They walk on trails outside the town and sometimes are disappointed when they realize they had everything they wanted where they live. Their bedrooms are much nicer than ours and over-all, they could be much more comfortable at home, instead of here.

But people are always looking for something precious that they don't currently possess.

But what if they already have this precious thing within them? After we worked through much of our trauma, Alesa and I realized that what we were searching for was already within us. It didn't depend on where we were or what we were doing. It had been there all along.

So, we say to ourselves, *I see your incredible preciousness.* And then we just smile. We smile because although we may have argued earlier when our ego got in the way, we can recognize the best in each other despite what's going on at the time.

This discovery didn't come when we were searching for it. It more accurately came to us when we were able to remove some egoic layers that kept it hidden. It was like peeling an onion and finding something beautiful underneath.

Beauty may be in the eye of the beholder, but treasure is in the heart of each person whether we do the right things or not. Our preciousness is inherent, not developed.

My hope is that everyone finds this treasure, or eventually realizes that they actually ARE this treasure.

6. People make mistakes

Several of our friends are less than perfect. They all have different personalities and abilities, but all have made mistakes. Some of these mistakes are at the level that I can't share them with you. I have made similar mistakes and regret the lost time and hurt they caused me and others.

But, if we are ever going to live successfully with other human beings, it is imperative that we learn to accept people the way they are. We shouldn't ever let people repeatedly hurt or abuse us, but when they make a mistake, we can't shame and judge them into submission. It never changes them and sometimes we lose the relationship.

I mention this because there are probably a few things that I realize now are things that truly make the world better. I once thought *love* was finding the perfect

person and living the rest of your life with them in
eternal bliss. But what I discovered was that love was
accepting another person that has flaws and makes mistakes, yet because of the commitment, both of you move
past the offense and grow and forgive and find a deeper
union.

It's the same with *compassion*. Everything in us wants to
judge and punish those who don't act the way we expect
them to. But the right move is almost always to exercise
some grace and compassion for them and even give them
more than we think they deserve. It is this compassion
that changes the world. Only when someone is seen with
eyes of grace, will they ever get better. Punishment very
rarely changes anyone for the better.

I hope that whoever reads this manuscript doesn't have
the mistaken impression that I ever was perfect or pre-
tended to be that way, I made so many mistakes as a
young adult. Operating from my ego was where I learned
all the lessons and mostly learned what not to do.

I also hope that people will understand the most important concept that explains what life is about.

Life is all about unselfish Love.

It always has been and always will be. If it's not about
love, it is most likely in vain. Many of the other words
that matter like forgiveness, compassion, mercy, grace,
joy, peace, kindness, etc., are essentially subsets of the
supreme command to love. It may be loving others, it may
be loving enemies, and it may be loving ourselves. But
it's all about love.

I hope that you have enjoyed what I had to say in this
manuscript. I could have written just as much about
choosing the right wine or managing a staff or getting

along with town people. But I don't think those things
matter like what I have written here. Look past the gram-
matical errors and listen with your heart.

I think you will find some treasure here, but ultimately
the treasure is in you!

—George Popper

WHAT HAPPENED TO EVERYONE?

MOM

FOR 20 YEARS, BETTY LIVED HER LIFE TO THE FULL. Someone was always with her at every meal, pouring their heart out while she loved them and listened to them. A few of the busybodies had changes of heart and came to renew their friendship with her which, in turn, had a positive impact on the church.

Because of her history, she had a unique perspective on suffering and boundaries and how much people need love. Her funeral was one of the biggest ever and held at the town meeting hall. People came from all over the region to pay homage to her.

Before she died, she was able to travel to several foreign countries and to some childhood dream destinations. She dated a few gentlemen but was never interested in settling down. When asked if she would meet a certain older gentleman, she would always say, "If he's lucky," but deep down she knew those men also suffered, and she was able to help many of them heal from their trauma.

GEORGE AND ALESA

GEORGE DIED IN 1969. TOWARDS THE END OF HIS LIFE, he was known for his generosity in the community. Because he was subdued and introverted, he was harder to approach than his mother, but his funeral was also epic.

Alesa continued to run the hotel until later in the 70s when the new interstate diverted the bulk of the traffic. She died 11 years after her husband. In many ways, she lived through the hotel. Her energy pulsed through the heart of each room. She never reconciled with her parents even though their negative energy drove her to change the most.

The couple never had children even though their staff adored them and worked until the hotel was sold to new owners. Many of the awards in the time capsule room were dedications of sorts from the employees to the couple. They treasured and loved them all.

Their businesses were eventually sold. As with many small towns, things declined and changed but the spirit of the couple lived on. If you look close enough, you can still see the original name of the hotel on the old sign. And, if you are brave enough to go inside, you might feel their presence if you believe in such things.

JOE AND MARY

THE COUPLE CONTINUED ON MOSTLY WITH THEIR ORDI-nary lives. They learned more about the modern process called focusing and shared it with friends to help them heal from their own trauma. Joe wrote a book and shared the principles in the manuscript by George.

Their lives were enhanced by the hotel and the things they learned from George from a previous era and George from the library. When he asked the librarian and people around town about the gentleman, they gave him blank stares and couldn't quite remember who he was talking about. He eventually stopped asking, and he never saw the man again even though he thought about him often.

Occasionally, when Joe was deep in thought, he would see him in his mind just standing there in his overalls. He wondered whether that was what Marla saw and tried to connect it all together, but it didn't ever make sense and didn't really matter. He did believe a bit more in ghosts, but he didn't fear or get too excited about them.

MARLA

MARLA AND HER HUSBAND CONTINUED TO WORK ON THE hotel until they were unable to do so. The time capsule in the basement became a museum of sorts that was open a few hours a day and on the weekends. Some other town history was included, but the focal item was and always will be a booklet called, "What Life is All About" by George Popper. Collectors from all over tried to buy the mint condition truck in the basement, but all agreed the building might collapse if they attempted to remove it.

EPILOGUE

THIS STORY OF *THE HOTEL* IS INSPIRED BY THE STORY OF a real hotel in my hometown of Rock Port, Missouri, previously called *Hotel Opp*. There are a lot of rumors and secrets surrounding the hotel. It is common for many to agree there were tunnels under the streets, but no one has ever seen them. There are also rumors of gangsters and ghosts, but many people dismiss that all together. If I had a million dollars, I would probably excavate the ruins and make it into a tourist trap. Or maybe not.

The legacy of the real hotel is like the legacy of the one in this story. When I asked about George Opp, the motivation for the character in the book, I only heard endless praise. Most residents that have distant memories about the hotel, remember not so much about the hotel, but about the owners. "They were decent people," I heard repeatedly. "They did a lot for the community," I heard from others. Either they were trying vehemently to overcome negative parts of history, or there was truly a legacy of a life well-lived.

I know in my heart that George (Dode) and Daisy Opp were possibly prone to take shortcuts in life, just like J.D., George, and Alesa were. What made them different was that they had the courage to face the difficult parts of their past and find healing and rebirth for their current lives. This allowed them to inevitably be life-giving to others and create a legacy for them to aspire to. The hotel had its day and was probably spectacular, but our story is yet to be written—to some extent.

Joe and Mary, in the novel, are based loosely on yours truly and my lovely spouse. We, too, have done the hard work of facing those *shadow* issues and now are able to serve as guides for those who also have the courage to do the necessary work. That is the legacy that we hope to leave. Laura and I run an organization called *The Desert Sanctuary.* We lead a contemplative experience called *The Being Journey* and one-on-one sessions like what some characters in the book experienced called *focusing.*

If you are ever in Rock Port, Missouri, look us up, and maybe we could give you a tour of the old Hotel Opp. I can't promise you'll see a ghost or discover anything paranormal, but you never know. At the least, you could buy some fireworks out on the highway and imagine the book coming to life just as I once did.

The hotel is now called *Cedar Bluffs Lodge,* and it is operated by Larry and Diana Liess. Diana appreciates the stories of the past, and the mystery is wrapped up in most small towns. The hotel has some magic to it which no one knows for sure where it comes from.

Thank you for going on this journey with us,

Be where you are, be who you are, be at peace!

—*Karl Forehand, 2021*

www.KarlForehand.com

For more information about Karl Forehand,
or to contact him for speaking engagements,
please visit *www.KarlForehand.com*

Many voices. One message.

Quoir is a boutique publisher
with a singular message: *Christ is all.*
Venture beyond your boundaries to discover Christ
in ways you never thought possible.

For more information, please visit
www.quoir.com

CPSIA information can be obtained
at www.ICGtesting.com
Printed in the USA
BVHW030017140322
631382BV00001B/39